Town of Angels Christmas
A Tale of Love and Animal Rescue

Jody Sharpe

Publisher: Jody Sharpe

ISBN: 978098856235

Cover Design: Jody Sharpe

Pasture Scene Photo: Liz Weir

Back Cover Design: Jody Sharpe

Originally published in the USA by Jody Sharpe

Katherine (Kate) Cameron Zara 1976-1995

"Just Live"

Words my late daughter said to me in a dream, March 2021

"I have seen things so beautiful they have brought tears to my
eyes Yet none of them can match the gracefulness and beauty of a
horse running free."

Author unknown

In Memory of Kate

Our Gift from God Our Joy

Chapter One
Past And Present

Flying at night is sublime. No human can see me. As the light rain stops, my feathered wings are beaded, but not soaked with rain. I fly this cool September summer eve knowing little hints of autumn waft in the air with tomorrow's promise of more golden days ahead. I am Angel Kenneth Heart, the largest angel of seven, having a human experience now. I've taken the name, Ken Leighton, a former football coach hailing from Africa, living in Mystic Bay, California, the town that mirrors heaven in so many ways. Tonight, as I fly toward my favorite big city by the bay, San Francisco, I think about the secret in my town, a secret well-hidden even though some have questioned it. Seven angels live as humans there. Wishing all humans could fly especially tonight as the rain stops this end of summer night, I fly north through the sea mist towards the wharf of the city of my heart. Flying makes my own angel heart alive with anticipation. Heaven has sent me on an angel mission tonight to help a homeless man on Bay Street.

As I come upon the magical city, the Golden Gate's lights glow in the night. They remind me of Mystic Bay at Christmas. Our decorations and Christmas Eve parade have gathered many from near and far. Angels appearing to three children and the angel-like spirit in Mystic Bay have people calling us the town of angels. Little do they know that seven of us angels actually live as humans there with our families. The secret, so far, is safe. I myself have a son, Val, who I adopted, but he really is the one who adopted me.

Above the glistening waters of the bay, my white wings flecked with gold fly hurriedly towards Bay Bridge Street. With gentle wind on my face and my angel intuition I spot the man named Walt. No one can see me as I swoop down and land, my wings disappearing at my side.

Sitting on the sidewalk in a thread bare t-shirt, Walt, though a young African American man, looks much older than his thirty - five years. He holds a grey, thin puppy. They both are abandoned and alone, shivering in the night. I place my jacket over Walt's shoulders and appear in front of him. He seems coherent and doesn't seem surprised to see me. My wings have disappeared, he isn't afraid.

"I'm here to help you Walt, to take you to a shelter I know, Bay Star Shelter." Walt looks up at me perplexed, and says, "The shelters I went to won't take this Little Guy. I found him on the street alone and hungry. So, thanks but I can't go in without him."

"I'll help you and take Little Guy home with me to Mystic Bay, it's only thirty miles from here. I'll keep him well until you feel better again. I'm going to get you some help, Walt."

Walt looks up at me seemingly surprised now. Then he studies me carefully. "You look familiar. You look like the coach from Africa, the one years back from San Francisco Shakers football team." I start to reply but he continues, "I used to go to the games when times were good, when I didn't have nothing to worry about, when drugs didn't try to kill me."

"Yes, I was the coach from Botswana and left ten years ago, Ken Leighton's my name." I give him my hand and he gets up slowly. I take Little Guy and place him under my arm. "Things are going to change for you now, Walt. You'll see."

We walk the few blocks together without a word in the cool mist of night. I volunteer at the shelter like many others living in Mystic Bay. As an angel, I can't change anyone's mind or future. Our angel mission here on earth is to comfort, console and guide people toward good. Now that I've chosen a human experience, I can do more daily interacting with friends and the community. Even if they don't believe in angels, eventually, most we encounter find their way to a purposeful loving life. "I want you to talk to Ronna the director of Bay Star Shelter. Like her mother, Mama, before her, she has programs for you and I will come see you once a week and bring Little Guy. I'm sure we can help you find a new start to your life."

Walt looks at me with the sunken eyes of months of neglecting himself. "Thank you," he says sincerely. "Coach, can I have the dog back when I'm better? I call him Little Guy!"

"Of course, you can."

After Walt is registered and Ronna takes his hand and says, "Come on Walt, we are your home for as long as you need it." Walt pets Little Guy one more time. And as he walks away, placed in the warmth of the shelter with Ronna's kind and loving care, I know he will improve. I send him angel wind with my hand. I see his shoulders relax; I see his step improve. "I'll see you in a few days. Now rest and take care," I call after him.

Walt turns and says, "Thank you. But Coach, how did you know my name?"

As I close the door, I wave answering in a whisper so there is no way he nor anyone else can hear me. "I'm an angel."

Out in the cool of the night the rain is gone. I look around, making sure no one can see me fly away. Holding Little Guy close, I turn and carefully ascend into the night. Over the street lamps and lighted tall buildings of the city, I fly with the puppy in my arms. Little Guy is unafraid as are all animals when they are with the angels. Little Guy is painfully thin and in need of a bath but he relaxes in my arms. Of course, I send angel warming comfort through my hands. Only those that have been touched by angel wind can fly. Yet, most only remember it as a dream. "Good boy," I say softly holding him as my white wings soar in the misty night towards the town, miles away, that I have called home for over ten years.

My son Val will love taking care of the pup for Walt. Our old dog, Barty, died a few months ago and we miss him dearly. Little Guy rests his sweet head on my shoulder. As we fly the stars in the misty night shimmer like diamonds as it gets cooler. We leave the bright lights of San Francisco behind. Toward the scattered lights of suburbs ahead, I decide to fly low as I approach Mystic Bay over old Zeke Lumberton's farm. He's left the earth for heaven just a week ago now. But his twenty-acre farm is up for sale. Retired vet, Doc Lindley, whose farm is next door, is planning to buy it from Zeke's heir and nephew, Dern, if the price is right. Doc has retired attorney Klaus Waxman and talk show host, July North investing in the venture to hire helpers and expand Doc's rescue of animals. He's got fifty plus deer, a few sheep and a horse now and wants to do more. That's what townsfolk do in Mystic Bay. We help people and animals in need. We celebrate others. I fly past Zeke's farm house. Sadly, no light on any more to welcome a passerby or flying angel like me. Doc and Shari Lindley's porch light is on at the next ranch over. There Doc sits in his rocker like he does each night. His old recued German Shepherd dutifully sits by his side. He gets up, stretches and walks into his house with the old dog trailing behind. Many nights as we angels fly by, we see him turn out the light and go in. It's a gentle reminder of the people and their peacefulness, the goodness of old in Mystic Bay.

We angels let the humans live their lives and choose their days. We are just here living as humans experiencing friendship, and family life, guiding with the gentleness of persuasions. Once we come down to live as humans, we grow old with the rest of the folk. I guess I'm about forty something in human years, but over four hundred in angel years.

My angel human story started years ago. I came to Africa to start a soccer team in Botswana and then Kenya. Then, Heaven sent me to California to help the football players on the San Francisco Shakers. There was a lack of sportsmanship and the team was flailing. Angel Taylor came with me to take a job with the San Francisco Shakers, as an accountant. We decided to stay and live a human life for a long time in the USA. I'm lost in thought thinking of my coaching days when I sense we are being followed in air. Is it a fellow angel or a bird?

I turn my head to look but a small screech owl comes by, passing me on the right. The owl with little white legs is flying ever so faster than me at a speed not known for owls. Amazingly, the owl looks at me briefly. He's communicating with me to follow him? We trail behind the owl now as we near the welcoming street lights of Main Street. We fly over Mystic Bay's heart-shaped bay where boats are moored and small lights shine on the water. But the owl's heading straight down Main Street. Since my house is but a few blocks away, I follow. It's odd to see a small owl fly down Main Street where no one is about and the mist has rolled in from the sea. I check on the puppy. Little Guy's eyes are closed, safe under my arm. I've soothed his mind and body with angel wind and whispers of love.

"Well, I'll be," I say out loud, the owl flies through the upper window of the apartment above our local pet store, Dear Dogs Etc. A woman stands at the window holding out her arms taking him to her gloved hand and then into an embrace. With my angel acute hearing I hear her say, "Boots, where have you been?" The light from within catches the beauty of her face. The sight of this woman brings a memory I can't forget. It was Christmas Eve and she was an eighteen year old, twenty plus years ago. I take in a rapid breath. Black, long, wavy hair with touches of light surrounds her high cheek bones. The sight of her is interfering with my flight and I'm starting to lose my buoyancy. Hastily, I turn around swooping so low I almost run into midnight walker, Jamie Bond and his trusty dog, Bondo. Oh no! I just miss hitting Jamie. I fly as fast as an angel can toward home disappearing into my own second story bedroom window. Bondo's echoing barks follow me. Jamie laughs, "You're always watching for angels, aren't you boy? Good night angel," he waves not looking up at me, knowing that Bondo does indeed see angels. Of course, humans can't see us, but animals? Oh, they see us, every one of them sees every one of us.

I recognized the woman in the window. I came to help her on an angel mission once just months after I came to San Francisco doing heaven's work with the Shakers. I was an assistant coach then and volunteered to help the homeless in town. She's Jordana Briggs. How could I forget her gentle grace, her lovely face and spirit?   I've wondered for years how she's fared and never thought I would see her again. Her guardian Angel, Claire, communicated wordlessly once Jordana was making her life a successful one. Angel Claire told me I would see her again one day and I so hoped I would through the years. And, here she is in Mystic Bay staying in the apartment above Gabe and his daughter, Hannah's store. She, of course, is the vet, Angel Doc Josh told me was coming, yet he never said her name. All angels can remember every human being and animal we have helped along the way. But Jordana, well, the young women caught my heart. And she has an owl companion? Of course, for she is obviously sweet natured and loves animals.

Chapter Two
Christmas Twenty Years Ago

I can't sleep which is odd for us angels having a human experience. We love the feel of rest. It's the wee hours of the morning when I finally get into bed. Little Guy had to be washed and fed. Our rescue dog Honey, welcomed him with a wagging tail and a sweet lick and I am holding the puppy next to me warm and snug in the covers. Honey is at the foot of the bed.

I don't need to turn lights on to undress into my pajamas or read at night, yet tonight I do so the dogs can see each other. Turning out the light I look out my window at stars shining. The sea mist breezes in. I close my eyes wishing for angel human slumber, anxious with questions of how I will handle Jordana living in Mystic Bay. I realize I've succumbed to the human feeling of anxiety, a new experience for me. The more angels live as humans, the more human emotions they feel.

When I met Jordana I was an assistant coach living as a twenty-two year old human but she saw me as an older man that night. Luminous Angel Claire appears in my room. Silently she communicates to remember the day vividly. She relates how Jordana has seen Angel Claire in her dreams. She reminds me she foretold the day would come when Jordana would be back in my life. Angel Claire sends me a wind of love through the wave of her hand, then disappears as the misty remembering comes. I now can see every detail as if watching a film.

Jordana Briggs is sitting at the City of LA bus station on Christmas Eve, an old suitcase by her side. Her plethora of coal black wavy hair is in a long ponytail. My heart sinks, for she's been crying. Her clothes are hanging off her. She looks painfully thin. I take the seat next to her and have manifested into the look of a sixty something kind and bearded African American man in a neat suit. I use a cane to steady myself, "Hello young lady," I say as I sit beside her. Jordana looks up wide-eyed and a little scared at first but sees I'm a well-dressed man and her look changes into acceptance. She herself is part African American and Native American from her mother's side she tells me later. "Do you mind if I sit next to you as it's the only seat available?"

"No, go ahead," she says in almost a whisper. Jordana looks down again. Her long eye lashes wet from tears.

After a few minutes of silence I inquire, "Where you going, if I may ask?"

"To San Francisco," she says.

"Oh, me too," I say now knowing she will be going and I shall follow. I am here to help her.

Silence keeps us just sitting for a few minutes until I say, "Going to visit someone for Christmas?"

"No, I'm starting college. I got a scholarship at Daily Community College and I can move in to the dorm Tuesday after Christmas." She half smiles.

"No one could take you? This bus station is no place for a young woman so late at night and your alone on Christmas Eve?'"

Jordana looks down, "My Aunt kicked me out of the house now that I'm eighteen. She gave my dog away. I don't know where she took him and I've nowhere to go till my college opens Tuesday. She starts to cry and I feel so sad for the poor young woman.

"I'm so sorry."

"My aunt gave me money for a bus ticket, told me to never come back. I couldn't ask my boss at the diner to take me. He's too busy at Christmas and I'd be embarrassed." Jordana is more than troubled and heaven tells me what to say. "That was so unkind of your aunt to do this. What is your name, dear?"

"Jordana May Briggs."

"Mr. Hart," I offer my hand and we shake hello. Angel Claire, her guardian angel, is nearby, her long blonde hair and beautiful blue eyes have tears for Jordana. She sends love through angel wind to Jordana and Jordana's shoulders relax.

We walk together as our bus is called and as if anyone would assume, she is my daughter or niece. We find a seat together and I know Jordana feels comforted by my presence as we ride the hours to San Francisco. It is then she tells me some of her story, filled with sorrow. Angel Claire fills in sending the words Jordana can't say. Her parents died, one after the other, of illness and her father's sister, her aunt, Marla, had custody and took over when Jordana was twelve. "My mother, Elmerine, was from Oklahoma. She was African American and Cherokee. She was an orphan and left a boarding house when she was eighteen, just like me to start a new life. My mother took a bus to LA to find work. She met my dad when the fire department was called to her building. She was going part time to college. Then, Angel Claire whispers to me the parents married and Jordana's parents were great people but they both fell ill. "My mother died when I was six. My dad when I was twelve." Angel Claire fills in the rest of the story. Jordana's Caucasian Dad's life insurance left money to his sister to care for the child. Since her aunt was prejudiced and fake around Jordana, the abuse started after he died. Jake, her dad had no idea Marla would be so mean otherwise he wouldn't have left Jordana with Marla. Jake's spirit appears in the bus now looking sad but he knows I've been sent to take care of his daughter.

Elmerine had grown up in Oklahoma but since she was mixed race she was looked down upon. Angel Claire shows me the great name calling and prejudice her mother faced in school and in town. She shows me the horrid Aunt Marla calling her a racist name. I see Jordana coming home from high school and her Aunt Marla telling her she gave her dog away. Where? The miserable aunt wouldn't say. I see Elmerine now, her spirit tearful for her daughter. I assure her parents' spirits wordlessly that now I will make sure she is safe. That is what angel missions are for. Both Jordana's parents' spirits touch Jordana's shoulder with ultimate love, then they disappear.

Jordana turns to look as if she knows the parent's spirits are nearby. Angel Claire continues, there was no trust set up for Jordana, just savings of her father's left for Marla to take care of her. Jordana felt she couldn't complain to anyone about the cruel ways of her aunt. Marla would tell her friends how she had to take care of the brat and her horrible dog. But Marla used the money to care for Jordana on herself. Jordana had to get a job at fifteen at the diner to buy food for herself. Her kind boss, Jim, at the Last Stop Diner helped out and the counselor at school helped her apply for a scholarship to Daily Community College.

"I have sixty dollars in my purse. My aunt never gave me anything. She put me down for being a different color." Jordana starts to cry softly.

It was as if Jordana had never had a soul to talk to about this. I said quietly with an ache in my angel heart, "How hard for you to lose your parents, and dog and have such a horrible person in charge. I am so sorry, Jordana."

"I'm going to college now to start a new life. I know my parents up there are proud of me. Sometimes I feel them near." By the last few hours of the bus ride Jordana grew weary. I sent angel wind to calm her from my hand as I gave her a handkerchief and said, "Believe in angels, Jordana. The angels are surrounding you. You are strong and God and the angels will protect you, they are with you always."

"Thank you, Mr. Hart. You know, I see a pretty angel in my dreams. Someday, I'm going to help animals. I hope to be a vet."

"How wonderful dear. I would like to get you help when we get to San Francisco, so no worries now." Jordana placed her head on my shoulder then and eventually fell asleep. I would take her to Bay Star Shelter where Mama, Ronna's mother, was director then. She would help Jordana.

The memory of mist ends. As I close my eyes, I think how the rest of the story ended. When we got to San Francisco, I called Mama at Bay Star Shelter. It was early morning but the sweet woman answered no matter what the time of day. I told her I met

Jordana on the bus, her story and inquired whether she could stay the days until the college opened and if she could go with her and settle her in the dorm. I know Christmas at the shelter is so comforting with volunteers serving good food, small gifts and singing. I told Mama to call me Mr. Hart not Ken when she sees me and Mama, though surprised, agreed. Jordana and I walked the several blocks to the shelter with the soft street lights decorated for Christmas. Mama saw me as young Coach Ken Leighton not the older Mr. Hart as Jordana did. My angel dust can transform me if I want any time. Mama and Jordana sat down. "Thank you, Mr. Hart," Jordana said. She suddenly stood up and hugged me tight. "I will never forget you."

"Mama will take care of you, then take you to college. Here is money to help you with clothes or whatever you need. Now go and show the world what Jordana can do. And Jordana, Merry Christmas." I smiled at her and thanked Mama. As I walked out of the door, I could hear them clearly with my angel hearing.

"Mr. Hart sat next to me at the bus station. He kept me safe and rode the whole way from LA with me. He is really a nice man."

"He is that," said Mama. "One Christmas angel of a man!"

Through the first two years of her college, I'd give money to Mama for Jordana. I never saw her at the shelter since I was so busy and only volunteered once a month. The last I heard Jordana graduated and received a scholarship to a Midwest college. "She has a bright future with an amazing healing touch with animals," Mama said. "When people would bring animals in, I would call her to take them to a shelter. The shelter would always tell me the animals arrived safe and healthy. It was amazing because some of these dogs and cats would be pretty hurt or ill." I didn't ask further as Angel Claire said now were the years for Jordana to really bloom on her own. "Your paths will meet again one day."

I so hoped and prayed for her over the years. All I know now is something's been missing in my life as an angel living a human existence. What's been missing is seeing Jordana again for myself, knowing she is just fine. And now she is indeed a veterinarian and living in Mystic Bay! I close my eyes and peaceful slumber comes with Little Guy in my arms and our Honey breathing softly, lulling me to sleep.

It's Saturday morning the sun is out, the dogs are fed and Val is at the Sports program. I'll pick him up with Little Guy after the appointment with Doc Josh. I'm nervous in Beach Tales Animal Hospital waiting room but the vet tech calls me into a room. I hope I only see Josh and not Jordana. I have to keep away from her somehow, I don't want her recognizing me. Why I wonder am I so anxious?

"Hello dear Ken. Who have we here? "

"Little Guy," I answer. "I went on a heavenly mission last night, helped a guy named Walt Bowen and took him to Bay Star Shelter. I'm fostering the dog for him and going to work with Walt down at the shelter. If it goes well maybe get him a job here in town when the time is right."

"Oh, wonderful, Ken." He checks Little Guy over. "Well, this fellow is so cute. Really emaciated though." As Doc examines him, I wordlessly tell him. Your new vet, Jordana Briggs, I helped her years ago on her way to college. I materialized into an older man. I hope she doesn't recognize me.

Wow, Ken are you sure? Her name is Jordana Hart. She was an assistant professor at Kansas State Vet school. Wait til you see her healing touch. It's way beyond what angels can do. She says she prays over the animal and God does the healing.

As Josh administers the shots and looks Little Guy over, my stomach is in knots. It's her I know it is. The door opens and there she stands. Jordana looks radiant. Her beautiful black hair is in a ponytail as I remembered, her skin, the color of coffee with a touch of cream, sets off the deep brown kindness in her eyes. It's her heart that captured mine that day long ago, her heartfelt determination when life had given her so much sorrow.

"Hello, I'm Jordana and you are Ken, Josh's friend. Nice to meet you."

She doesn't appear to recognize me and so I relax a bit. "Yes, hello, Doctor Hart." I say her name wondering if she took my name when I posed as Mr. Hart that long ago day.

"Call me Jordana, please. Let's see your Little Guy. Whoa, look at those paws. "He's going to be Big Guy!" She laughs and runs her hands over him. "He needs fluids, Josh, don't you think and his paws are raw."

They administer fluids and I watch as Jordana lays her hands on each of Little Guy's paws. The soreness is leaving. Wordlessly, Josh initiates silent angel communication.

You see what I mean Ken? She is a healer.

"Jordana, Ken believes in spiritual healing as so many of us do in town. I told him you have abilities."

"It's all work from above. I pray over each animal." She smiles, leaving the room telling me again how nice it is to meet me and she will call tomorrow to check on Little Guy.

I sigh.

Josh says," What's wrong, Ken? She didn't recognize you. Oh, I remember that one guy recognized you last year at the angel debate. He remembered you helping him by the side of the road years back. He thought you were an angel." I remember again with the misty film in front of my eyes. "He looked like you, Coach!"

"You handled it with angel dust. You can do it again if necessary."

"No. The man recognized me because I looked like myself. But Jordana saw me with very different appearance, grey beard, with a slight limp."

"That's good, then no worries. I have news about the horse rescue tomorrow at four, come to the house. We are having a meeting with Bobby Delaney about Zeke's ranch sale. We have an update on the fence, and Dern, the nephew's, got a problem with the price on the ranch. Timing is crucial. There are twenty-two draft horses in Nevada that need a home. Jordana and I need to get a horse here for medical reasons according to Jim, the farmer. We will take him to Doc Lindley's farm but I can't leave the practice if she's gone. Do you think you could drive her there and bring her back towing Doc's horse trailer? Also, Andy asked if you could be in charge of the rescue operation cuz he and everyone else is swamped. I know you are busy, too, but you've got help at your store. Could you take it on?"

I sigh again. "We angels should not be in charge of anything in town except our businesses and helping volunteer. We have agreed we will not take on political or committee heads. The townsfolk need to learn to lead with only a touch of angel guidance."

"I know but since he asked for you specifically, can you just do it? We need to pick up the horses by December seventeenth, if we get enough horse trailers and the deal is done by then."

I ask, "Do you think angel dust will do the job to soothe the horses or will we need meds for them?" What I don't tell him is I'm driving two hundred plus miles with Jordana alone. Oh my, how will that go?

"I don't think we'll need meds now that we have Jordana Hart. She has the ability to calm animals to almost sleep walk. She is thrilled to help. Meeting her at vet school and her coming here to live at just the perfect time for us to move the rescue horses, well it is meant to be, God's work."

"Yes, yes," I say. Josh has more patients so off I go to pick up Val and surprise him with our foster dog. But as I drive, I wonder what it will be like to drive with Jordana to pick up the horse. I'll send lots of angel wind of forgetting if she seems to recognize me.

Val is both an ecstatic little boy and a sad one. "I'm sorry," I say to my son hugging him. "We are fostering and when the nice man feels better, we have to give Little Guy back."

Val looks down despondent. I put my hand on his shoulder. "He found the dog. What if Honey was lost and we were sick and someone helped find her for us? We would want her back, wouldn't we?"

"I guess," mopes Val. It's sad because as we arrive home dear Val has already bonded with Little Guy. "He's a Pitbull right, Dad?"

"Yes, a mix of Pitbull and he's going to be huge. Look at those paws!"

When Sunday arrives Val and I are in my angel store Heaven Can't Wait. Val is playing with Little Guy in my office and taking him out for potty breaks on a leash. I'm unpacking the Christmas angels, ready to put up more shimmering Christmas trees in the store as soon as October blows in. The lovely psychic, Justine, walks in my store. Not only is she my across the street neighbor and next door store neighbor, but I am her guardian angel. Of course, she doesn't know it. I've sent her butterflies for years to help this precious person and amazing artist all her life. Butterflies are calming just by sight. She recently married after losing her husband a few years ago and Val and I are so close to her and Mac, her husband and little Billie Jo, their granddaughter. Justine sweeps over to me a kiss on my cheek. "Hi, Ken. Bobby will be here in a sec with the new vet, Doctor Jordana Hart. He's her realtor and he is smitten. She is not only beautiful but so nice." My angel heart skips a beat. We talk a little and then good looking Bobby Delaney breezes in with Jordana in front. I almost drop the fragile glass angel ornament worrying she'll somehow recognize me now.

"Hi, Ken, I hear you've met Doctor Jordana Hart."

"Hello! Yes, we've met."

Jordana says hello, seemingly in complete awe looking at my store. The scrubs are gone and she wears jeans and oddly enough a sweatshirt with an angel on it. Her shiny hair is long to her waist and I have to look away to avoid making eye contact. "Oh, my Ken, I saw Justine's beautiful Painted Butterfly store and now I am here with all your glorious angels. Look at all the Christmas trees with ornaments. This is heaven to me for sure. I love angels and butterflies."

"Please take one of your choice," I tell her. "Everyone who comes in gets a free ornament if they want." Val comes in from my office holding Little Guy. "Hey, Justine, can I go over to your house to show Billy Jo the dog?"

Justine replies before I do, "Of course, sweetie. Mac and Billy Jo are home. You got a new dog? How great! What's his name?"

"Little Guy," Val says proudly. Before I can say anything Jordana walks over to Val. "Hi, I'm Doc Jordana the new vet. Little Guy is going to be a very big guy but I know you'll take care of him."

Val looks down. "He's not really my dog. We are fostering, my dad says until Mr. Walt can move here."

"How nice of you," Jordana says her hand on his shoulder. "I had a dog like him once but, well, it's hard when you can't keep a dog you love. Val, how about you pick a pretty ornament for me?"

Val walks over to the white flocked Christmas tree, "Pick this, it's my favorite!" The angel on the ornament is holding a little dog in her arms.

"That's the one," Jordana beams. "Thank You!" Val looks pleased and takes Little Guy out the back door to see Billy Jo just across the alley.

Jordana says, "I'll see you later at the meeting, Ken and we will be off to get the horse in the morning, correct?"

"Yes, that's the plan. See you later."

She says as they leave, "Thank for the lovely ornament." She smiles. "I'll be back to shop in both your stores for sure."

"Goodbye," Bobby says." Justine and I say goodbye. I smile heartily knowing so far so good.

A customer comes in and I greet her. As she walks around Justine stands back clearly wanting to catch me alone.

"Ken, I have a question for you."

"Sure, what is it dear?" I am perplexed now as a worried look has come over her face.

"Bobby wants to ask Jordana out but he's unsure of himself after that last disastrous girlfriend so I told him he should send her a letter to Beach Tails Animal Hospital. But what should he say? You are always so good with words.

That line you wrote for my sign in the window yesterday, A Butterfly is a Tiny Angel, has brought more people in. You have a way with words." I look away and out to the street at the people passing by. The customer is looking at a sign I wrote with angels, stars and moon on it. Invite The Moon, The Stars, The Angels in To Your Night. I think of something to say but it sounds too romantic. I write it down on a piece of paper anyway.

I'd like to get to know you. Would you take a walk with me down Main Street? Let me show you our town of angels at night.

"Wonderful." Justine says reading it. "You helped me write my advertising so many times." She kisses my cheek and almost flies away back to her beautiful store, all things butterfly. I see my Justine happily married to Mac. Her joy is my joy. The customer interrupts my train of thought wanting to buy a beautiful angel statue. After she leaves, I sigh, yes that would be good, a date with Bobby for Jordana. So then perhaps I can get on with my angel human life and not worry about her realizing who I really am. Why, I wonder, did she never marry?

The night is cool when Val and I set foot in the cozy house Gabe, Aunt Helen and Hannah, Josh and their twins live in. It's a wonderful house behind the alley of their store. It was Hannah's late grandparents and great grandparents, the Dear family's, feed store long ago.

I'm thinking how I love having my human earthly life now with the other angel friends and human friends too. Jordana is here and I can watch her life grow but from afar. Maybe she'll find love here with Bobby. Why am I feeling a human feeling they call melancholy?

Chapter Three
Seven Angels And The Horse Rescue Team

Gabe meets Val and me at his front door. All angels will be in attendance as committee members today. Bringing Val into the kitchen, we see Aunt Helen, Gabe's sister in law, busy getting our refreshments ready. Val goes right to the kitchen table with Josh and Hannah's little twins, Hannah, their mother, is making cookies with them. The pinkest kitchen ever is so fun to look at… retro everything. "I could smell those cinnamon rolls down Main Street, Helen!"

"Dear Ken, so glad. I made them just for you all with your hearty appetites." Aunt Helen laughs as Bubbles the tame squirrel jumps on her shoulder.

Aunt Helen hasn't learned the secret yet and Gabe, Hannah and Josh hope to keep it that way. She goes along merrily cooking, keeping house, attending garden club meetings and babysitting the twins while joyfully loving each day. Gabe's companion squirrel, Bubbles, keeps her company all day long hoping for a morsel dropped on the floor or better yet, he's an excellent catcher.

As I go back to the living room, Angel Taylor Msumba walks in greeting everyone. I've known Angel Taylor for four hundred years, we worked in Africa then with The San Francisco Shakers.

We greet each other with big bear hugs as our bond is close. He is married with two little girls now.

Klaus Waxman walks in, a burly man who's perhaps the kindest of all humans in town now. Klaus came to town a few years ago challenging the angel sightings in town. He acted like a real bully. Yet, July moderated a town event called The Angel Debate and it proved to be a turning point in Klaus' way of thinking about the existence of angels. I taught him as much as I could about angels in our counselling sessions. Wonderful things happened in his transformation. Klaus became a different man, set free one would say, to find the peaceful meaning in the life he craved. Andy Walin and Jamie Bond walk in. Andy, the Mayor's son, runs the towns' dog and cat rescue and owns the hardware store. Jamie Bond, owner of Bondo's Bikes, matured with the help of the late Madam Norma and her daughter. Jamie and Klaus? Well, they are both Comeback Kids as we angels call them. Both have grown spiritually thanks first and foremost to the kindness of my dear, departed friend, Madam Norma. They are good men, doing good for the community.

Next sisters, Angel July and Angel January, walk in with their children with happy greetings for all. Their angel story is a miracle itself to tell. Our seven angel bond is a strong one and of course, all of us have children now. July and January have each adopted also and have made Mystic Bay their home. July does her worldwide TV shows now in Town Square, weather permitting. They take their kids into the kitchen as Angel Donnie comes in. He owns with his wife, Laurjean, The Next Door Café. "Best food in town," Laurjean's Miss America sash says as she scurries around taking orders.

Klaus, Andy and Jamie are talking and so wordlessly I say to the angels present, The woman I helped long ago is Jordana Hart, the new vet and will be arriving soon with Bobby. So far, she doesn't seem to recognize me as the old man who helped her years ago.

Gabe communicates, this is the first time someone we have helped has moved here. But Ken, you looked so different to her then so don't worry. When my daughter, Hannah, told her ex-boyfriend years ago that I was an angel, well, that's when we worried. But we made it through with the help of the town. If she questions you, we are ready.

I communicate, The world must not know yet that we angels live among them.

The angel communication stops as July speaks to all of us. "My October TV shows are focusing on mending the broken fences of race in this country. My guests will have inspirational stories to tell. Then in November, I want you to know that I will have animal rescuing as each shows' topic ending with the rescue of the horses coming from Carson City to old Zeke's place. I am so excited about this everyone!"

Bobby Delaney walks in with Jordana. I see the way he looks at her and I take in a deep breath. Everyone is introduced and each angel wordlessly communicates to me how lovely Jordana is. Doc Lindley walks in the house last and has already met Jordana.

I rise. "Hello everyone, take a seat please. I'm taking over the head of the committee as Andy has asked me to. I hope that is all right with you all. If there are no objections, I will continue."

"Of course, there are no objections," says Josh. All the others nod or agree.

"Thanks for doing this," says Andy.

"Thank you, everyone. Jordana Hart and I are leaving tomorrow to bring one of the horses who is ill back to Doc's farm for treatment. We will be checking on the other horses as well. So perhaps now is a good time Jordana for you to tell us how you will help on our rescue horse mission."

Jordana rises. "I am a large animal vet and used to teach at Kansas State where Josh and I both graduated. He asked me to be his partner as Doc is now totally retired and there is a huge need growing here. Of course, I was drawn to the angel sightings history of the town. I do have a method of calming animals on a spiritual level. Maybe it doesn't sound so strange amongst such an enlightened group as yourselves. I will try my best to calm the rescue horses on our journey home to Mystic Bay. I am so pleased to meet you all." She sits down and glances my way, a sweet smile of friendliness on her face. I nod and smile. It's clear there is not one ounce of remembering on her part. I do not seem familiar to her and this makes me glad. I am so proud of the woman she has become.

"Jordana, thank you." Jordana looks lovely, wearing black jeans and shirt with yellow stars on it. Her hair, long to her waist, shines by the light of the lamp she sits next to.

Andy speaks next. "I have a lot of work to do for the rescue to happen but I am working on securing the seven horse trailers needed and negotiations with the farmer taking care of them now. He needs to be paid. I know we can make it happen. Thank you to all of you who have donated money to feed the horses til then."

I say, "Thanks Andy for all you are doing. Bobby you are next up with the update on the sale."

Bobby stands but looks overwhelmed for a moment. "Well, unfortunately, Zeke's nephew is playing hard ball. He wants more money than the generous offer Doc, Klaus, and July have put together for the sale for the proposed rescue ranch. He's touted he can get a higher price and has one coming. Are we at a limit ourselves financially?" Bobby sits down and I watch Klaus, and July look at each other. Next door neighbors and partners in securing money for the sale, the way they look at each other now tells me there's a spark of romance.

Doc Lindley speaks up. "I am definitely at my limit. Incorporating the two rescues into a charity is a blessing but where would we get more money? We've had fundraisers and asked so many to help. How much more does the greedy guy want?"

Bobby seems worried, "Five hundred thousand more." The room is silent. But July speaks, her kindness and beauty standing confident. "I can ask for money somehow from my contacts. I know it will take time though, I need to really think about who to approach."

Klaus states, "I'll find us another place to rent for the horses temporarily. Give me that job and I'll do it."

I speak up. "Okay, thanks Klaus and July. We have a plan but we have only eight weeks left til we pick up the horses. Tomorrow Jordana and I will drive to Nevada and bring back the horse that is ill. How about ten Jordana? Twenty Moon Road, the late Madam Norma's Parlor?" She nods yes.

"Klaus, you are pretty sure you can find a place to rent?"

Klaus has emotion in his voice, "You all accepted me and forgave me with kindness and when I apologized for my horrid behavior. I want to do whatever I can for the town, the horses, my friends. I will make it happen and pay the rent myself. It's just, Bobby how can this sale ever go through now? Do you see hope of any kind?"

"Not really," says Bobby.

"Let a few of us meet with him." July communicates wordlessly now to the six angels. Remember how we all helped Klaus' turnaround and his belief in angels solidify. Maybe we can do it again with love, with a committee of kindness.

I admire July's idea but it was different circumstances. Klaus was a sad, confused man with alcohol issues. For all we know Dern is just greedy.

Gabe says, "Yes, let's bring him here next meeting a week from tonight and try to convince him. That is if you can, Bobby, and of course, make sure he brings his real estate agent."

"He's an attorney too," Bobby says.

"I'm not afraid of that part," says Klaus. "I'm an attorney and so are you." Everyone laughs albeit nervous laughs but this all makes me sad for the horses. And I'm driving to Nevada with Jordana tomorrow alone? It's like heaven wants us close and so be it. I will handle it. The secret is what it should be, a secret. I send angel wind to all in the room. I notice all the angels doing the same. Smiles come on the other committee members' faces. Bobby smiles at Jordana and she smiles back but then looks at me and smiles. I look at Angel Gabe and he nods. What's that about? I pop a piece of cinnamon roll in my mouth and laugh watching

Andy grab another roll and twirl it slowly round and round just like Bubbles the squirrel.

Chapter Four
20 Moon Road

I've been a counselor at twenty Moon Road for many years. As I wave goodbye to Walt's first session at Moon Road, I remark to myself what a blessing I asked Klaus to be Walt's other mentor. I watch them drive away as Klaus takes him to his new apartment. I feel so proud of Klaus' change to a man of greatness. Helping the town, using his own money to rent a farm for the horses is a wonderful gift. His kindness is never ending. I think about how life has changed for Klaus and now Walt. Walt and Klaus' lives are so similar in story. Jamie Bond has offered Walt a part time job fixing bicycles at his store, Bondo Bikes. Walt and Jamie have lots in common too besides a love of bikes. Jamie matured under Madam Norma's love and counselling a few years ago. Walt will stay in Jamie's shop for a short time. A small apartment in the back of the store with a bed and bathroom and tiny kitchen are all he needs. Jamie will make sure Walt eats meals with him.

 "More tea and banana bread, Ken, for your road trip with the lady?" Mabel calls to me from entry hall.

"Yes, thank you Mabel." I pet King who leans against my leg. Sometimes I want to just take him home with me as our bond is so profound. He and I see Madam Norma's spirit together now. King looks up at her with loving eyes and I too, find tears of joy at the corners of my eyes. The smart, kind woman looks younger than when she died. Her favorite blue dress almost sparkles in the morning light coming in the window. She disappears and King lays his head on my lap once again.

Warm and caring Mabel brings me sliced breads to go in a bag. "Ken, I made enough for you both and two cheese sandwiches so you don't even have to stop for lunch."

"Thank you, Mabel, you are dear to so many." Mabel shines with kindness and appreciation.

"Ken, King and I love when you come over twice a week. "

"Me too, my favorite times of the week.

I sit on the couch waiting, tearing a little piece of bread off for King. I hear foot fall coming up the walk.

When the doorbell rings, Mabel answers it and surprisingly King doesn't bark which is his usual greeting.

"Hello, I'm Jordana Hart. I'm to meet Ken Leighton here."

"Yes, yes, come in," says the sweet Mabel with King now by her side now. "This is King, he won't hurt you." Jordana sees me and smiles and bends down to greet King. "Hello Mr. King." She touches his head and the dog of course can feel the love and healing hands. "His arthritis is acting up. I'm a vet. Do you mind if I run my hands over his legs?"

"Oh, no, of course, please do," says Mabel.

"Hello, Jordana, this is Mabel Anderson and now you two have met." I smile at Jordana and she smiles back. Her long hair is swept to the side in a pony tail and her smile is infectious.

Mabel stands back. "You remind me of an old friend of mine from so many years ago when I was a teenager. You are quite the spitting image of my friend from Oklahoma!"

"Oklahoma? That's where my mother was from! Tulsa?"

"Oh my, could you be Elmerine Smith's daughter?" Mabel studies Jordana and holds out her hands.

"Why yes, I've never met anyone who knew her then." They are holding each other's' hands and looking at each other and I find myself speechless.

"We both lived in my grandmother's boarding house. My grandmother died suddenly and my uncle said everyone including Elmerine had to leave. I begged her to stay with me but, she wanted a new life. I wrote her a few times and then we lost touch. Oh my, God and his helping angels must have sent you here. Where is she? Is she here with you?"

Jordana has tears in her eyes now. "No, Mabel, Mom died a long time ago when I was a child." They tearfully hug each other.

Jordana pulls away for a moment. "You are May May? Everyone called you that at the boarding house? My mother gave me your name as my middle name, Jordana May!"

Mabel and Jordana are crying and hugging. "This is so wonderful for you both to find each other. You two sit in here and talk. I'll go outside for a little while. I have to thank the angels for this remarkable happening!" Jordana nods and I take King out to the backyard into the beauty of the bejeweled garden. We sit under the Bishop Pine and I feel my heart sing with joy for Jordana and Mabel. A reunion meant to be.

Chapter Five
Horses In Need

Jordana and I are in front of Zeke's twenty acres with its many shade trees waving in the fall wind. The green and brown pasture surround its old clapboard farmhouse. We hitched the horse trailer on and now feel the wind blow east as we get out and stand at the fence admiring the peaceful scene. Jordana looks to the sky, then closes her eyes. "The horses will feel love here. They will be happy and the town will be happy, too. More goodness will come."

"Jordana, may I ask you, are you psychic also, or do you feel only what the animals feel?"

"I feel their illness, emotions, but, no, I'm not psychic about humans. I only can tell if I am well received." She smiles a half smile. "Are you psychic, Ken?"

"Oh no, just a father and friend to anyone who needs me." I smile and the answer seems to satisfy her. "Because you have a phosphorescence about you, a light within that glows. I noticed it. In fact, even Josh has a little. I thought maybe you both were psychic like Justine and Hannah."

"Well, no, that would be nice, though."

We are quiet now and the quietness seems to linger. Neither of us wants our thoughts to end. The wind is warm on our sun-filled faces. I break the silence, "Shall we go?"

Jordana nods and we get in my truck and gaze for a moment, saying goodbye to the farm house and acreage hopefully soon to be home to the horses. Jordana starts the conversation as we ride. "Tell me about the children who saw the angels a few years ago. I know two have to remain anonymous, but I've heard only bits and pieces."

I tell the first story of Emma Rose, Jamie's daughter, yet I do not say her name. "The first child was six at the time, a girl with intellectual disabilities. She and Madam Norma's great granddaughter, Maggie, were picnicking behind the little girls' home. The child with special needs was mute until she saw an angel. She exclaimed, "Angel" to the surprise of Maggie, her babysitter that day. Maggie, witnessed the miracle of the child speaking for the first time. But Maggie didn't see the angel. However, she did see the spirit of her beloved late dog. It was a miracle and thus began the sightings. She first told Miss Marilyn and Madam Norma. They formed a group to decide how to handle the news for the town and the world."

"That is so beautiful. Tell me more please."

"Shortly after that, an anonymous little boy also with special needs had visitations from the angels and drew and painted two impressionistic canvases of angels as well as if he was a student of Monet. The first children will remain anonymous always but the third child, Benny Chen, with a visual disability, had angels visit him while sleeping. He heard them whispering a song he should play for the world. The boy has played it for Presidents,

Kings, Queens and as many folk as possible. His father is in the San Francisco Orchestra. His talents are rising.

"The museum in Riverton is where his song Forever Love Forever Peace is played over and over as visitors walk through viewing the paintings of the boy and the story of the formerly mute little girl. Everyone calls the song The Angels Song. A documentary plays every hour produced and filmed by Maggie's' husband, local writer, Noah Greenstreet. The town has changed. A zero growth bill has passed so there will remain a small population of seven thousand, but the surrounding towns are thriving. Riverton is booming to the east with the Museum there as well as Millersville to the northeast. It's economic progress and providing a good living for many who need good wholesome towns to raise their families."

"Ken, this is all so wonderful. I'd heard of miracles in a California town and when Josh emailed me, I knew I must have been waiting for just the right time to move back to California. Angel sightings, kind people, animals and the ocean are all the things I love."

On the way to Carson City, our conversation changes as Jordana speaks of Mabel and how finding someone near and dear to her mother is like finding real family in Mystic Bay. "The angels made it happen, I know. All my life I prayed for someone who knew my mother and here she is right here in this quaint and friendly town where miracles are happening!"

"It's wonderful, Jordana, truly wonderful and the angels must have surrounded you with love. It was meant to be."

"Someone else said those very words to me long ago. You remind me of him."

I try to change the subject. "Oh, the miracles that have happened in Mystic Bay, Jordana and with the horses coming soon, well, what a blessing."

Even though I've tried to change the subject, Jordana starts to tell me the story of the angel who helped her long ago.

She relays the story with sweet remembering. "The man you remind me of, well, his name was Mr. Hart and I never saw him again after that Christmas Eve twenty years ago. I left my aunt's home at eighteen. She gave me a bus ticket and pretty much said to get lost. I had a scholarship in my suitcase, sixty dollars and a few clothes. I was scared and alone at LA's bus terminal but Mr. Hart, a kind African American gentlemen, sat next to me the whole ride to San Francisco. He asked if he could sit with me, but really what he did was protect me the whole way there. I told him my story, including I had nowhere to go until school opened after Christmas. I was running to nowhere. My confidence was nowhere, too, but Mr. Hart took me to a wonderful place, Bay Star Shelter, the same one some of the people in town volunteer for. Mama, the director took great care of me, and during those days I grew to appreciate her kindness. Mr. Hart left money for me for school and clothes. Through the years, I tried to find him, but I never knew his first name and Mama, didn't, either. He was so kind and dear I would like to find him to tell him thank you again, how I worked hard dedicating my life to help animals. You know, Ken, I haven't told many my story. I will tell Mabel, though, and you. You are like him, kind and gentle. Although, he was much older than you." Jordana looks out the window at the landscape speeding by.

"I am happy Jordana, Mr. Hart was so kind to you."

I am praying to God, to please not let her figure out I'm that man, that angel, for I fear it will ruin her trust in me. She will think I've deceived her. Would it ruin her memory of that fateful day, the helpful, Mr. Hart, an older gentleman?

We arrive in Carson City to the small farm housing the twenty-two draft horses. It's atwo acre place with a run-down barn, but plenty of feed for the horses. Doc Lindley, July and Klaus and our supporters have supplied the farmer with everything he needs to keep the horses safe until we can pick them up December seventeenth. A very old farmer, Burt, is in charge. He needed the money so he rented us the place temporarily. But he is selling the land. We get out of the truck.

"They eat a lot of food. I need another check if you don't mind." Burt and I are talking and he doesn't notice as Jordana walks in the gate with the horses. Her essence and love swirl in the gentle breeze like the beautiful horses' lovely manes. Her hands are outstretched, and, remarkably, the horses are coming to her one by one to feel her energy of love. I try to concentrate on the farmer talking to me but can't. They nudge and love on her, these twenty two massive horses, each one beautifully different colors of chocolate, autumn and gold and white, with manes flying up in the breeze and steady eyes on Jordana. Today, as their eyes concentrate on the genuine love and healing Jordana brings, they have no agenda. Jordana is sending them pictures of their new home to them and they are understanding.

She leads Star into the horse trailer. "This other horse needs to go with Star. They came together and are inseparable." "Of course," Jordana says, leading then the other gray thin horse into the trailer. It's as if the horses are indeed sleep walking. I send angel wind to all the other horses to feel peace and loved. I send butterflies, too. The horses seem to love the swirling small group of butterflies touching them ever so lightly. Burt seems to respond to the angel wind and butterflies, too. I notice him closing his eyes and calmness comes on his weathered face.

Jordana puts her finger out and a yellow one lands for a moment, then flitters away. I write out the check and hand it to Burt. I know that Klaus has offered more money to Dern Lumberton for the farm. How much Klaus and Bobby won't tell us but if the deal falls through, we are to take them to Millersville where Klaus is trying to rent the dilapidated farm Doc's deer came from. No matter which place, these horse's future will be good. These neglected beautiful creatures have found their advocates in Mystic Bay. Jordana, this spirited vet, this healer of animals, has been heaven sent.

Jordana and I say our goodbye to our charges. We wave to Burt. Jordana is reluctant to go as we drive out the dusty road. "They are comforted now knowing they will be moving, that we will be back soon to take them to their new home where they will run free. They know I had to take Star and the gray mare. Oh, Ken, they are such beautiful spirits each and every one!" Jordana looks out the window of the car at the high desert scene and we are quiet as the dusty road ends and the highway begins again. She turns toward me, "I think we should name them each a name associated with Christmas!"

"A fine idea! Let's have the committee's children name them."

"Tell me about you Ken, where you were born, about your life in Africa."

I tell her the truth. I don't mention my birth, but tell her I was in my late teens in Botswana and loved sports and started a soccer group for all ages.

"Were you born there? "

"I'm not sure of my birth place or the year."

"Star has a wound on her leg and hoof that must be dealt with pronto." She starts praying in a whisper for the animals behind us. I send my angel wind too but some must have fallen on her for she falls into a light slumber, her head against the window. I feel more peace now as I drive in silence, the two hundred plus miles toward home. She wakes as we are drawing near Riverton city limits.

"Oh, Ken, I fell asleep, I should have helped you drive. I'm sorry."

"I love to drive, it's fine." I look over and smile at the loveliest of faces.

"I feel the horses in back are just fine. We can do this mission, our big rescue drive of twenty now horses to Mystic Bay. I think Star and Noel, I just named her, feel your kind heart, too."

"How nice of you to say."

"I've known you forever it seems. You are so easy to be with." She pauses. "Do you mind me asking you about Bobby? "

Uh oh, I think. "Of course, please do."

"He asked me out in a lovely note. I said yes via text. He called me but it was so odd. He said I stared at you at the meeting, so he wondered if you and I were dating. I said no, that it's just that you remind me of that old man who helped me long ago."

My heart sinks, what do I say to her. I try to act nonchalant and chuckle a fake laugh. "Old guy?"

"Seriously, you have a way about you. We are connected." Her eyes are on me, I know, but I keep my head toward the road. "Yes, Jordana. We are connected to the horses and to the miracles of the town. We are blessed with good, helpful, loving natures." That statement seems to satisfy her and there is no more talk of connection. We talk about the drive to get the horses and the timing to get the horses to Zeke's ranch, how it will be a small miracle considering the demands of Dern Lumberton. As we drive into Doc's driveway with the medically fragile horse and pal, I don't tell her that last night as Val said his prayers, he looked at me with hope in his big brown eyes. "I asked God to send you a wife and me a mother."

Taken back, I composed myself, "You did, son?"

"Oh, and to please make it Doc Jordana."

Chapter Six
The Angel's Way

I haven't seen Jordana this week. I've been busy at the store and the sports programs but maybe I'm avoiding her. I should have called and asked how Star and Noel were doing. It's our committee meeting night again. Zeke's nephew, Dern, walks into our meeting as Angel Gabe opens the front door of his house. He's handsome, about forty, and struts in like he owns the place. Behind him creeps his real estate agent and attorney, Sidney Deever. They are both dressed in expensive suits. "Well, well, well, the great committee I hear trying to talk me down on my price. It won't work, you know. I'm Dern Lumberton, Zeke's fav and only nephew." He sits down on the couch without being invited and Gabe looks aghast at his behavior. Josh, Gabe, July and I, the only angels present, sit along with Doc, Bobby, Klaus and Jordana.

"Mr. Lumberton, Mr. Deever, I am Ken Leighton, head of the horse rescue team hoping you will sell to Dr. Lindley, Mr. Klaus Waxman, and Ms. July North." They nod as each is introduced. "Our other committee members, Andy Walin, Gabe O'Ryan and vet Josh Ryder." They nod and say hello. "This is Gabe and Josh's family's home. Also, this is veterinarian Dr. Jordana Hart, our guest tonight, and a large animal vet." Dern can't help but stare at the lovely Jordana. "Of course, you know Doctor Lindley's real estate agent, Bobby Delaney.

"There are refreshments here if you would like, tea and coffee and water and the town's famous, Aunt Helen's cinnamon rolls to share." Andy eyes the cinnamon rolls and takes one. I would chuckle but this is an important meeting.

"I will start this conversation. Dr. Lindley and his partners, Ms. North and Mr. Waxman, want this sale to go through as you know. You have been offered over the amount that you and Mr. Deever initially came up with. We have twenty horses coming from Nevada, hopefully, before December seventeenth when the farm they are lodged in is sold. Since we are approaching November we need the horses in the ranch by that day, no later. Zeke's ranch will be a 501 (c) (3) charity. So, would you like to speak to us first? The committee, who will be the prospective board members of the charity, would like to share their thoughts."

"There's no need for anyone but me to speak. I've already decided on the price and I stand firm with it now. My uncle wanted me to have the ranch and it isn't anywhere in the will that I have to sell it to a rescue organization. Right Sid?" Sidney the puppet like real estate attorney nods, "You are correct, sir."

He turns to Jordana, "By the way, don't you recognize me, Jordana, from Daily Community College? Years ago, I met you, but you never gave me a second look. A big mistake, I must say." Jordana decides to be silent and I applaud that. We all ignore him but Aunt Helen almost waltzes in with more cinnamon rolls. Flustered, she stops in her tracks, blowing a whisp of gray curl out of her face.

"Oh my, you have hardly touched these? Okay, I'll take these warm ones back." But Bubbles has followed her and comes up to the table and swipes one of the rolls and starts to eat it round and round like Andy. I can't help but laugh at the witty squirrel and so do the others. Andy talks as if Dern never said anything to Jordana and it's natural for a squirrel to come in the room. With a mouthful of cinnamon roll, "Let's continue this meeting, please!" Aunt Helen laughs and says, "Come on Bubbles, there's more for you in the kitchen." Bubbles understands and hippy hops behind Aunt Helen through the door.

"Your town is weird with everything angel and squirrels coming into living rooms!" He turns to July, "How come you live here, July? Beings that you're so famous? I don't get you people."

No one speaks and the tension is so thick in the room, I can't help myself. As an angel, I can make myself appear larger to anyone I want and no one else will notice but angels. For Dern, I grow another foot slowly and my brawn is brown and massive. Dern looks at me and seems a bit unnerved. Attorney Sidney seems to shake a little. Bobby speaks up. "As a realtor and attorney, this sale needs to happen for these animals. Doc Lindley has kindly offered to oversee them. If you can't find it in your heart to help by sealing the fair top notch deal with Doc, July and Klaus then we have no need for further discussion. Do we all agree?" Everyone nods or says yes, even Doc who is saddened by this whole process nods then gets up and walks into the kitchen.

"I'm not intimidated by any one of you. My price stands. Double the offer or I will find a new buyer. Come on Sid. Let's get away from these angels from nowhere." He starts to walk out of the room eyeing me with some fear with Attorney Sidney trailing behind like a duckling after Mama duck.

July stands. "Sit down please, Mr. Lumberton. I have something to say."

We all look at each other. "Plan B," Andy says so only I can hear.

Dern stands defiant and I can tell Sid wants to run out of the room. "Mr. Lumberton, your uncle, Zeke, was a dear man. All his money was tied up in the property. He and your Aunt Beatrice lived a frugal life with joy and love for their few rescue animals. Doc Lindley took them in and has been paying for their food and medical needs. The whole town would like the horses housed there as your uncle would have loved the thought. He told Doc Lindley personally he would like it to be a rescue after his death. And if he never stated it in the will, well, Dr. Lindley and other friends will swear in court, he wanted this and said so!"

"I don't really care what the old man wanted. It's mine now, and I'll do what I want."

July is frustrated but Klaus begins and he again awes me with his composure, his kindness, wit and persuasiveness. "We have found another place if you don't take the offer but our hearts for the animals are set on your Uncle Zeke's place. Doc can oversee the animals, and the town will be thrilled and we all will move on. But you know," he says shaking his finger at Dern, "You remind me of the old me, the man I used to be, the man I'm embarrassed was me. But this town changed me. Angels appeared here to little children. People are kind here helping children and animals less fortunate. The noble thing to do would be to help us reach a settlement. Take this overly generous offer or we WILL take the horses elsewhere."

Dern is silent.

The next move is the way the angels move. I announce, "So before we adjourn our meeting, we welcome you to please stay. Gabe and Josh have invited us all to drink and eat the best cinnamon rolls in California and quench our thirst. Lemonade, tea, coffee!" Ignoring the two insensitive men, we all take turns taking drinks and rolls and Doc walks back in. But Dern seems furious he hasn't caused a confrontation. We are ignoring him. "No deal!!!" He and his timid attorney leave the house.

"What's next?" Andy says.

Klaus has been thinking. I know him. I counselled him when he came to town with that same bullying nature of Dern's. He speaks up and every one listens to the retired successful attorney.

"I promise Doc and everybody. I have a place for the horses. I'm on it and will get it ready for them hopefully by the seventeenth." July looks lovingly at him.

"Thank you," says Andy. "But please, let's eat these rolls before Bubbles comes back." We all laugh, but I'm looking at Jordana. Being confronted by Dern couldn't have been easy for her. I step over to her.

"Jordana, are you okay?"

"Yes, Ken. Thanks. You know you do remind so much of…." Bobby notices we've been talking; he comes over to us. "Jordana, shall we go on the rest of the walk down Main Street?" Bobby looks at her and then at me and I smile.

"Oh, I am tired, Bobby, but thank you, really. Excuse me please, I want to see Bubbles and the kids." She walks away and we both watch her go.

"You know Ken," Bobby says almost in a whisper." She's one of a kind and wow, so beautiful and she's healing my dogs' arthritis. You are so good with words and not interested in her I'm sure so can I ask you what else to say to her?" I know what Bobby is doing. He's letting me know hands off. Instead of not giving him words and thus being unkind I say, "Tell her in a note how you feel. "You are heaven's gift to the town." I smile again at Bobby.

"Thanks, Ken, I will write it tonight. You are the best. I'm glad you aren't interested." Bobby gives me a big pat on the back and I find I can't blame him. Jordana would be any man's angel.

As Bobby walks away, I wonder if he senses something in my persona. Is it evident? I've never had a date even. Do I stare at Jordana? Probably. I will have to watch that. The secret has to be kept at all costs, especially since she would know then that I was Mr. Hart and that can't happen. Will July, at some point, tell Klaus the secret that we are angels? He once asked me if I was one. Everyone is eating and talking now about the horses and how Star and Noel are doing and Klaus' prospective place to rent for the horses, the Millersville land, but I'm remembering my conversation with Klaus when he gently asked me the question, I couldn't lie when responding. The memory is there in mist glittering once more….

We are standing on Klaus' patio looking out at the waving sea…

"Ken, I've asked you before, we all have a guardian angel, you are sure of it?"

"Yes, I really do believe it, Klaus."

"And you think Madam Norma and Freddy, my dog, and Tyrone, my cat, are always with me?"

"I'm as sure as rain falls, that is true."

"Have you seen Madam Norma's spirit?"

"Why yes, I have, but only for a moment." He is asking me so many questions and of course angels never lie.

It's then he says something to me that makes me almost disappear from sight. It happens to angels when they are overwhelmed with sadness, humanly fear or surprise. And right now, suddenly, I am a little fearful. I feel my wings urging to sprout and nervousness sets in.

"I believe you are an angel, Ken and that you don't want anyone to know, I believe God sent you here to help Val and me and so many others. I watch you. You almost glow and somedays you actually appear bigger. That man, Cliff, at the angel debate? He said you were the spitting image of the man who helped him on that dangerous curve years ago. You laughed it away but I could tell you were visibly shaken. And then at the Town of Angels TV Show when he was interviewed, Cliff didn't mention how the man looked like you. He totally glossed it over. You are well known so why didn't he say it? It was strange".

"He told us all he thought the man who helped him had to be an angel. Why, I've wondered didn't he bring your name up on July's TV show? It got me thinking about you. Could I be right? Could you tell me? Are you a real angel? I'd never tell if it's true. I promise. It would help me so much to know for sure."

"And that day when you showed up at DiMaggio's bar in the morning. How did you know I was there? Did you fly there?" He turns to me again. "Madam Norma said you know more about angels then anyone, she said also that you see them. Did she know you were an angel, Ken? I need to know."

I am speechless. I hold my wings back with my angel mind and they stop sprouting. I sit on the chaise across the balcony from him. I start to speak but he puts up his hand.

"Listen, you are the finest man I have ever known in my life. Knowing you are an angel would help me get through my life and it would be a secret I would keep. I swear." Klaus looks at me with tears in his eyes. Thankfully my composure comes. The Lord gives me the words.

"If I'm an angel, then I'm only an angel to some. It's an honor to me you think of me as an angel.

"Thank You."

It's then I see her, Madam Norma. She's smiling behind him, standing in a blue dress looking younger still. I see Lucky his dog and Dot his cat stare at her. In an instant she is gone. I decide quickly to communicate wordlessly to the animals to go to Klaus for a hug. Run, I tell them with my mind. Kindheart, his guardian angel, stands near to us now. He nods smiling. The dog and cat look at the angel and then at me and run over to Klaus almost flying into his arms. Klaus smiles and laughs at big Lucky almost bowling him over. He surely is about to say more to me but I send him angel dust with a slight wave of my hand. It covers him from head to toe with little silvery sparkles he can't see. Lucky and Dot see them and Dot unsuccessfully paws at them. Klaus closes his eyes then opens them again. Hopefully, the angel dust worked.

"What was I saying? Oh yes, I was telling you about my friend, Paul. Its indeed nice of you to help him. I know he'll learn so much from you. I was saying something else I don't remember. Oh yes, Madam Norma was like an angel!"   It's then the mist of remembering ends.

I look at Klaus now. The man I helped is helping the horses find a home. His goals have changed to one of helpfulness and peace. I sigh with happiness for Klaus and go into the kitchen grabbing a roll on the way.

In the pinkest kitchen on earth Jordana is holding Bubbles and Bubbles seems captivated by her. "Bubbles usually has to get to know everyone before hugs and kisses, but he loved Jordana as soon as she arrived," says the fun loving, award winning Aunt Helen. "He's happy and on your shoulder too!" Everyone laughs. Val is having the best time. Dad, we've been playing with Bubbles, Dawn too. Can we get a little deer like her too, Dad?"

"No, unfortunately son, but I'm sure you can come over anytime to see Dawn, right Aunt Helen?"

"Absolutely, Val. It's very unusual for people to have a deer as a pet. We got special permission to have her."

Jordana pipes up, "The twins see Bubbles and my owl all the time. Why don't you come up to my apartment with your dad now? I want you to meet my animal friends!"

"Can we, Dad?"

"Of course, son." My heart sinks. I don't look at her but fluff Val's hair on his head. I make myself look at her, "A little screech owl with little white legs, how cute. Can Val hold him on his arm as you do?"

Immediately I regret saying it.

"Yes, how did you know about my screech owl?"

I catch myself and smile. "Everyone loves animals here in town and well...."

Fortunately, chattering Bubbles does some antics for the kids, catching pieces of roll in his paws. "Goodnight everyone, and you too Bubbles!" Jordana says to all. We say goodnight also as we follow her up the stairs to her apartment. The studio apartment is very Zen and soothing. The little owl is perched on a cat perch. The calico cat, Kashi, lies on another perch. They both look at us nonchalantly.

"Wow," Val says excitedly. "Can I touch them?"

Jordana laughs, "Yes, but ask them first." Val asks Kashi first before petting her. Boots is next. Val manages to give a pet to Boots' head. The owl closes his eyes.

"These are fine animal companions. Tell us how you came by them."

"A colleague at work found them playing in a field near her home when I lived in Kansas. They were both young and Boots was feeding Kashi, the kitten, little bugs. I named him Boots for his white legs and Kashi means Shining. I sat on the ground near them for the first few days with dishes of meat. Kashi came to me first. On the fourth day, I sat still and put my hand out to her. She took her paw and reached for my hand."

"How beautiful, Jordana. You really have such communication and love for animals. They trust you."

"Well, it wasn't long after that I started petting Boots. Finally, he let me pick him up after I coaxed him for a little while. I took them home and it's been a love match ever since." Val loves playing with the cat and Boots keeps an eye on us the whole time. It's funny how Boots looks at me. He communicates by a picture he sends from his mind to mine which shows me standing by Jordana. I am stunned. I announce it's time to get home to bed, "See you soon and thanks so much, we loved seeing Boots and Kashi, didn't we Val?"

"Yes, thank you," Val hugs her waist. I almost run down the stairs. Too much contact with her, gotta keep my distance.

"It's so cool, Dad. The owl and the cat play and sleep near each other. It should be a story in a book!"

"Well write it dear son of mine. It would be a great story to tell!" We walk home talking about the owl and the cat. How will I handle this? I could tell Jordana didn't want us to leave.

At home, the other six angels communicate to each other without words. Donnie communicates for us to fly Saturday night. July will babysit Val. But I let them know that I'm not up for flying Saturday but maybe next week.

As I get in my bed, I get a phone call from Josh. "What's wrong, Ken? Still worried about Jordana finding out you're an angel?"

"Yes, honestly, my love for flying has waned. I'm stressed, a totally human trait, and worried about Jordana finding out especially when we ride to get the horses. She'll have more questions and I won't have the answers."

"Maybe she's supposed to know you were her angel that night. Look, just sleep on it and talk tomorrow."

"Thanks Josh, good night."

I get up and go into Val's room and watch him sleep. What a good boy he is, snug with his dogs by his side. He has a surprise tomorrow. Walt says he's visited with Little Guy and he feels Little Guy needs to stay with Val. I'm proud of the growth Walt has made and Val, well, he will be over the moon with glee.

I look out the window across the street. Justine and her family are asleep in coziness. The street lights shine amber in the neighborhood. The moon is out as Bondo walks his human buddy, Jamie. I see Angel Taylor flying above, his beautiful rainbow wings shining as he sees me and waves. Bondo barks and I hear Jamie say, "Goodnight angel! Sweet dreams."

I turn in thanking God for Val and my life. I will solve my human-like stress somehow with help from my angel friends and from above.

Chapter Seven
The Offer

It's Halloween, I'm having breakfast with Miss Marilyn at The Next Door café. "Happy Halloween! The usual?" says Laurjean, Angel Donnie's wife. She wears a wild outfit, hair dyed green now with blue and green flowers on her polyester seventies' pantsuit, white sash that says Miss America and green tennis shoes. Her smile is as big as the blue green ocean.

"Wow, you look colorful as always," Miss Marilyn laughs.

"You do look wonderful, Laurjean, I mean, Miss America! Yes, the usual please."

"Gotta keep the patrons wondering what I'll wear next! And my hair color is always changing!"

"I'll have the Sunshine Pancakes too and plenty more of your great coffee," says Miss Marilyn. Miss Marilyn's eyes shine like her mothers' and for a moment I feel like I'm looking at the dearest lady and friend of all. Laurjean sashays away and I say, "You are so dear, just like your mother, Miss Marilyn."

"Wish I was as psychic as she was. Thank you, but I still got some vibe, Ken. Listen I called you here today to pose an offer!"

"I'm intrigued. What would that offer be?" Taking a few sips, I sit back to listen but it's crowded and I use my angel hearing over the crowd filled noise.

"Well, two things really. Tim and I want to downsize and live closer to our store. We want to trade houses with you if that is something you might enjoy. You have always loved twenty Moon Road and you do so much counselling there and Mabel would still keep house for you and us. This is if you think your son would like living there. We'd let Mabel have the other part of the duplex you own now as our gift."

I start to speak but she holds up her hand just like Madam Norma would do. "And dear King would finally be your dog. He'd stay, for he loves you as much as he loves Mother still."

I'm speechless for a moment then immediately know the answer, "Yes of course, I'd love this for Val and me but I'd have to confer with him. He plays every day with Billy Jo, but it's just walking distance to her house from yours."

"Great, let me know. Our houses are worth similar prices and Bobby could work out the details."

Our pancakes arrive and more coffee is poured by sassy Laurjean. "Enjoy people!"

We chat some more as we eat about the trade of houses and decide it sounds like the best plan for all. I notice Klaus and July have come in and wave to me. Then Donnie comes out of the kitchen asking how my pancakes are. Gabe and Hannah walk in with the twins and wave as does Taylor and Hattie with their toddler girls. This is unusual. All angels are here except January and Josh?

Then Miss Marilyn calls to someone just walking in the restaurant. I turn. It's Jordana dressed in scrubs, her high cheekbones in a smile, her hair in a long braid. Her essence shimmers as always.

"What a surprise," I say standing holding a chair for her. She sits. "Hi, Ken. Hi, Miss Marilyn," They   hug.

"Ken, I asked Jordana to stop by in case you have questions about King's staying with you if we have a deal. I hope you don't mind. But I have had the lovely opportunity to talk to Jordana a lot since she and Mabel connected."

"Of course. How are you Jordana?"

"Just fine, thanks." She looks at me but turns to Miss Marilyn who leads the discussion of King's mental health. Jordana assures us both King is as attached to me as Miss Marilyn and Tim feel. "Maggie will come over frequently and of course Mabel will be there too, and Tim and I'll stop in all the time. It will be like Grand Central Station, as Mother used to say, if you can take it, Ken." Jordana says, "It's actually ideal for King and you, Ken." She smiles though I see sadness in her eyes for a moment. Is it because I've been avoiding her? She asked us to come for dinner one night and have her famous Macaroni and Cheese and I begged off. I feel I am being stared at. And what are all these angels doing here?

Wordlessly, July transmits the angel's message. All the angels feel the same way. You need to ask Jordana out, Ken. It's synchronicity and serendipity in their glory. We all know you want to be with her but you! So what if she finds out you are the angel who helped her?

Oh boy, Angel Josh has told all the angels how I feel and I bet Klaus knows too. I'll have to talk to him about that. July smiles and I look away and take a gulp of coffee. I am starting to sweat and I thought angels don't sweat.

Jordana sees me looking off a bit and says, "Are you all right?"

"Yes, ate too fast I guess."

Miss Marilyn winks as she leaves and says, "This is on me dear Ken, I'll be in touch!" She puts money down on the table and leaves.

Jordana looks at me. "We need to meet with the committee, I had a dream communication with the horses."

"Well, look around most of the committee are here." I signal to Klaus, July, Taylor, and Gabe to come over to the table.

They all do and drag chairs over. Laurjean gets Donnie to come out of the kitchen to hear what's going on.

"The horses expressed fear to me in a vivid communication dream. They are weary and troubled. They are starting to lose confidence that we are really coming. They want to see Star and Noel again. We need to go there and soon," Jordana tells us.

Klaus says, "Okay, since there is no resolution with the offer on Zeke's property as of yet let's proceed. We must take them to the acreage in Millersville but it's not totally ready for them yet. If Andy can get the horse trailers to us by Saturday we can get moving."

"Okay," I say, "Is everyone on board?" They all say yes.

"Okay, I'll call Andy and Doc now. Gabe, you tell Josh. July you tell January and the committee will be notified. Seven am

Saturday meet at Zeke's place. Jordana, does Bobby know about your dream?" I hate asking about Bobby, but this is business.

"Not yet, but I will see him today and explain we are moving forward with the transfer. Maybe that will help the sale maybe not. We can't count on Dern."

My heart twists a bit. "Okay, I'll be in touch with you all when it's a go." I stand to leave, but the mental communication from July stops me in my tracks. Look Bobby is outside waiting. *You better move, Ken!* I quickly say goodbye saying, "I have to run to get ready for the annual Halloween party." They all say they are going. I'm sweating, irritated, sad and want to go to sleep. Human feelings are getting to me. I leave in a hurry waving goodbye almost running into Bobby. "Hey Ken, your love notes are working!" I feel like pushing him down! Oh, no, what's happening to me?

Chapter Eight
Onward And Upward

Val's happiness is my primary goal. Today is November first, fifty three days til Christmas Eve. The Halloween Party at the High School gym was fun for Val and all the kids and parents. I stayed busy giving out candy. Afterward, Val and I went trick or treating to Miss Marilyn and Tim's on Moon Road. We walked up the steps to the house I love greeted by granddaughter Maggie and her husband, Noah. Of course, dear King greeted me with his usual loving lean on my leg. Val hugged him tight.

My ten year old son never ceases to amaze me with his gift for friendliness. He said "It's okay with me if we move in here. My friends can walk here and I love this house cuz Madam Norma lived here. I want King to be our dog!!"

Tears were shed and Mabel had made Halloween cookies for us to share. But as we celebrated and after I showed Val which room will be his, the doorbell rang. It was Jamie Bond and Walt at the door.

Walt says, "Happy Halloween, Val. Hey, I like your great costume. You know, Christmas is coming and I've had many days of visits with Little Guy but I have to tell you, Little Guy loves you the best. I thank you for taking good care of him but it's time for me to say he is your dog, not mine."

Everyone was thrilled, especially Val.

"Really, thank you, Mr. Walt!"

We walked home and I dropped off Val for a night at Justine's to look over his and Billy Jo's bags of candy and probably giggle all night. I lie on my bed realizing Val has changed my life. I'm an angel having a human experience, or so I thought, but I am soaring in life with the most beautiful of human lives…a son, and a town I love. I'm helping God with His Earth in small ways. Jordana will never know I'm an angel and maybe marry, Bobby, but I will be okay. I have all I need. I have a basket full of enough. Don't I?

I close my eyes listening to the night. The slightest breeze from the window is lulling me toward sleep. The dogs by my bed snooze, but I realize someone is at my window. It's Boots the owl, staring at me sitting on the window sill. Come, Jordana, he communicates. I shake my head and tell him wordlessly. I can't fly anymore but Boots flies away. Jordana needs me but what can I do? I communicate to Angel Josh to help me. I go up on the roof steadying myself, concentrating praying for the ability to fly. My enormous wings emerge miraculously. Thanking the Lord, I soar high above the house trying to locate Boots in the night sky. He's there ahead and I try to catch up to him beneath the waning crescent moon and brilliant starlite. "Wait for me," I call!

Chapter Nine
Rescuing Man And Beast

My wings hurt. I haven't flown since Jordana came to town yet, I feel free again, flying toward where I wonder. Not to her home, not out to sea, but east. What's happened? The little owl just keeps flying speeding through the misty sea winds. We are going to Lindley's farm, I find. It's there I see her car speeding on the road near the farm. We fly above her but does she see us? I see Doc on his porch with his dog barking furiously. There is a man at the fence screaming. It's Dern. I fly down landing, wings still at my side. Dern sees me as an angel. I have no time to transform.

Dern is crying on the ground. He has paper which looks like a letter in his hand. "I have no one now!"

I send him angel wind. He calms, looking up at me, and cries out, "You're an angel! I send wind again and he closes his eyes. He tries to stand and I help him up, my wings disappearing as Jordana drives up. She gets out running towards me. Doc comes walking fast as he can with his dog by his side. Josh drives up behind her.

Dern looks at us all with surprise. He looks around for his angel. He doesn't know it was me. He's disheveled and has been drinking. Will he remember I came to him as an angel? Josh has walked up.

"Doc, I saw an angel! Ken, Jordana, an angel was here! He was big, black like you Ken!" He starts to cry uncontrollably. I communicate with July in my mind what is happening and to send Klaus now.

Dern is holding on to me crying. "Look at this letter Uncle Zeke wrote for me to find in his desk. It says you are all I ever hoped for but you never came by. I leave my homestead to you because I loved you."

Jordana closes her eyes in prayer for Dern, her hands are outstretched. Doc calls Bobby on his cell. I hold Dern in my arms sending angel wind through my hands, "Dern, it's okay. Your Uncle Zeke knows now that you are sorry. He loves you still and so do God and His angels."

As Dern still holds on to me, Klaus and Bobby drive up. Dern has somewhat calmed now from angel wind and my touch as he sits on the ground. Doc has brought him water. Klaus bends down next to him. "Dern what can we do, how can we help? "

"I saw an angel Klaus, big and brown like Ken with wings. He was twelve feet high. An angel came to me man, an angel even though I've been awful to this town, to Uncle Zeke, to Doc and the sale. I'll sell at your price. I'll sell like my uncle wanted me to. I'm sorry, please forgive me."

After a while of quiet talking, Klaus leads Dern to his car. Dern is in good hands now. Zeke's ranch will be home to the horses for sure. But one thing is also for sure, a man's life was rescued tonight. He saw me as an angel but will forget my face, but it changed his world like it does for so many. He will become a better man moving forward.

As he leaves Jordana turns to me with a quizzical look. "Ken, how did you get here?"

I don't lie, I flew here. Your owl came to me communicating you needed me. I hitched a ride with an angel of a man riding by."

She looks so surprised, "I did want to call you, but didn't want to bother you. Doc called me. The deer and other animals were spooked and that he heard cries. I drove as fast as I could." Bobby is overhearing all this and says, "Why didn't you call me, Jordana?" He's upset but Jordana handles it with softness. "Bobby, Ken and I are trying to get the horses here. We are on a team." Bobby says nothing and walks over to Doc to talk seemingly upset with Jordana. But I can't care about that now. The fact that Dern had an awakening is the most important thing now. We talk a while to Doc and Shari. Bobby leaves, telling Doc the deal will be done as soon as possible. He goes to his car without saying goodbye to Jordana as she offers to drive me home. She insists on driving me home. "Tomorrow is the horse rescue. You have to sleep."

"I know." We say goodbye to Doc and Shari and get in her car. "Why didn't you drive your car?"

I can't lie and so I say truthfully, "I just knew I had to go quickly and I didn't know where Boots was going. I went into the night as fast as my body could carry me." Again, my poor explanation seems to satisfy her. She says, "Dern will be okay, don't you think?"

"With all the angels in this town, he will for sure be just fine, Jordana."

The dogs are in the open window looking out anxiously waiting for me. They bark as I get out of her vehicle.

"Thanks, Jordana."

"I'll see you tomorrow, Ken." Her dark hair glistens in the light from the car.

"So glad for Dern tonight."

"And he saw an angel!" Her eyes are as merry as the star at the top of a Christmas tree. But am I really so glad she didn't think the angel was me?

Chapter Ten
The Angels and the November Sky

Jordana and I leave for Carson City with the others driving behind us, each with a horse trailer and an angel living as a human driving. The whole way we discuss Dern. Paul is staying with him today. There will be a plan for him, of course, to have rehab, counselling, doctor assessments, but mostly he will be surrounded with love to help him through this journey.

"Dern said he saw a big angel, like you! How wonderful and so magical. Ken, did you see the angel?"

"I think so," I say, not wanting to lie.

"I've seen mine in dreams. She's beautiful with golden hair and wings that are translucent. I can't see her face."

"Many can't," I blurt out wishing I hadn't said it.

"What do you mean?"

"Oh, I mean those who have seen angels say it's hard to discern the face of an angel."

Thankfully, she changes the subject back to Dern.

"It was so great you were there last night. I still can't believe you ran and hitched a ride."

"I was upset. I had to keep up to find Boots. I knew he wanted me with you." Jordana is silent then and I don't think she heard me. She is preparing her heart and mind for the horses. She will calm them enough to follow her lead and walk into the horse trailers.

Jordana looks at me. "It was heaven's plan I come here, Ken, to meet you, the townsfolk and help the horses. I know now the angels are real. I think I know now, Mr. Hart, the old man who helped me, must have been an angel."

I say to her with kindness, "I'm sure he was."

Chapter Eleven
The Rescue

The remembering comes in the daylight. As I went to bed last night, I heard the sound of the rustle of a wing. I looked up and there floated Angel Claire, luminescent with light hair cascading to her waist of gold. There also stood Madam Norma beside her in her blue dress with blue light around her smiling face. Madam Norma speaks to me, "Celebrate this life you have. Tell her tomorrow, Ken. It's time, for you have loved her for years. She will understand." Madam Norma is gone before I can sit up in bed. Angel Claire communicates wordlessly to send Jordana angel wind to calm her as you tell her. She has waited for you since the night on the bus. Angel Claire disappears.

My remembering ends. Jordana has been praying. She says as we get out of the truck, "Ken, tomorrow this miracle rescue will shine to the world."

We are all out of the trucks as Jordana stands and leads the horses. We angels send angel wind but Jordana is praying and talking and sending her own heavenly healing. The horses come to her two by two as if Noah from the Bible's story is here with her. "Come," she says, Come to your new life of freedom." In silence they move. Burt and all of us are mesmerized by the sight as the gentle giants almost float on air into the trailers. One by one they walk as if transformed into spiritual beings for a moment. The horses are in a sleep state as they enter the trailers. We angels know what will happen next and we are not afraid. As we say goodbye and start to proceed back, I try to get the courage to tell her the truth but I find I can't. Not now, not yet!

We come to the fork in the road. It is now I must try the angel wind on her. I hold my hand out and Jordana looks at me with questioning eyes. The angel wind has a sparkle to it and she closes her eyes and falls into slumber. I signal with my hand outside the window and the trucks and horse trailers raise as if Santa himself is in charge. On angel wind we propel up, up high in the air where only birds and animals can see us. As we fly above the roofs of the houses and dusty roads away from the highways, I smile. This is what it should feel like on Christmas Eve with Santa at the helm helping boys and girls of all ages have a merry Christmas and life. But we angels and kind humans need to be the Santas of this world to people of every color, race, religion and creed, for kindness is the first ingredient of love.

Chapter Twelve
The Courage Within

She's opening her eyes. Oh no, we are high in the air. I send angel wind and her eyes then close. She reaches her hand over to touch my arm. She is in a sleep state, yet not as deep as I hoped. "Ken."

"Yes."

"We are up in a plane?" Her eyes are shut.

"No, we are flying with horses in the trailer behind us."

I see her open her eyes looking out the window. "Pretty down there." Then Jordana, the heart of my heart squeezes my hand, "Your hands are so like my angel, Mr. Hart's hands." Her eyes close in slumber again. Relieved, I send more angel wind to her. I sigh now and remark at the beauty of the day below and the clouds above. We are doing God's mission, taking these gentle souls to their forever home where nothing can harm them. The town of Mystic Bay has wrapped it's love around the rescue of these horses.

We land with a few plumes of dusty waves at the outskirts of town where no one can see us. Traveling slowly into town, Jordana and Klaus in July's truck wake up. Jordana is rubbing her eyes and yawning. "I dreamed we were flying high with the horse trailer. I could even look down and see the road and town below."

"Wonderful dream," I acknowledge. We see the townsfolk lining the street. I called Andy from the air. "We will be early," I said. "No traffic on the way." Of course, there wasn't, we were in the sky. Many townsfolk are lining the streets but they have done exactly what we asked. They watch us in quiet jubilation as our silent parade of horse trailers pass down Main Street. The children's sweet voices are the only sounds we hear. Their voices are the songs God has written. People are sending love and good wishes.

It's late afternoon as we arrive at Zeke's ranch. Doc and Shari stand waiting. They have opened the fence to their farm so the horses can travel to and from the two places, a connection, a beautiful bucolic scene. Star and Noel grace us with their presence. Jordana has communicated with them that their family of horses are arriving. Star's leg and foot have healed and his countenance is grand as he stands waiting.

Jordana hasn't said much as we landed, still a bit groggy, I'm assuming, from the angel dust. She gets out and as the horses' stalls are unlocked, out from the trailers the magnificent ones come. They are still sleepy and so they walk ever so quietly into the pasture. Jordana leads them two by two, talking low but we angels can hear her sweet melodic voice of love reverberating in our angel ears. "You are here, free my loves, free to live. You are home." Doc, Shari and the rest of us are tearing up for we know what love can do. I see them, the multitudes of angels singing above. Some of the horses look up, for they can see them too. God is good, I communicate to my angel friends. In unison they communicate, Amen.

The trailers have left one by one. We will leave in Jordana's car but she is still praying over the horses with hands outstretched. Some have regained their wakefulness enough to snort and run with the light winds, neighing and nudging their soulmates.

I watch her, knowing this is the time I have to tell her. If she faints, I will catch her, if she cries, I will hold her. If she walks away, I will let her go. I am an angel living a human existence and I cannot let love pass me by. I must be brave for me, for Val, for my own angelness. I must celebrate and live this glorious chance I've been given. Loving Jordana has been an unexpected blessing of living as an angel human existence.

Jordana walks out of the gate and stands at the fence, watching the horses graze in their new home. The air is filled with the sweet aromas mixed with meadow grass and the horses.

"I felt so strange waking up knowing I slept almost the whole way home again but dreaming of flying. Strange, because Klaus said he slept and dreamed he was flying, too. But here we are, Ken! Look at this miracle." I can tell she is silently crying. I put my hand on her shoulder. She doesn't touch it.

"I don't want to leave here. God and His angels brought me here to witness this miracle of love."

I wait. There is silence, then she says almost in a whisper, "I got a call from Bobby last night."

I say nothing.

"Bobby said you wrote those lovely notes to me that he penned as his. He thinks you and I are in love. He said he will walk away and be happy for us. Are you in love with me, Ken?"

My composure almost leaves me, but I say quietly, "Turn around. Look at me."

She turns, her tear-stained face glows in the light of the sun nearly gone now as it melts below the earth.

"Jordana, I love you, yes. It was always you. From the moment I first saw you over twenty years ago."

Jordana doesn't move. "What?" There is questioning and some fear in her eyes.

"Don't be afraid, please. I am an angel from heaven's realm, living as a human here in Mystic Bay. There are seven of us who have lives here. Twenty- two years ago, I was sent on a mission to help you. I was Mr. Hart that night. I am Kenneth Heart, an angel."

Her face has a look of disbelief. Her tears have stopped on her beautiful face. "Mr. Hart?"

"That was me, Jordana. I've kept it from you because I didn't want to ruin your idea of your Mr. Hart changing your life. I wanted you to have that memory forever of the older man helping you like a father figure. I am sorry if this hurts you. I will go if you want. I know this must be overwhelming. I didn't know if I'd ever see you again but your guardian angel, Claire, told me we would meet again. And here you are and here I am telling you the secret very few know in Mystic Bay."

"But…you are an angel? Did Dern see you as an angel? Did you fly following Boots?"

"Yes, Boots came to my window. I followed him here. I saw your car. I was above you, but people don't see angels most of the time."

There is a pause then, "Can you, will you stay here, with Val?"

"Yes, I will grow old and when Val is of age, I will tell him the truth. Please, my love, come to me for you love me too, don't you?" I am getting choked up. She is not running to me as I hoped she would. We haven't even kissed. I don't know what more to say about my love so I say, "What you did for the horses today was angels' work."

Jordana holds on to the fences' rail as if she might faint. I reach out but she turns away again, then back.

In almost a whisper I say again, "Jordana, please reach for me. I'll be here forever for you."

Jordana let's go of the rail and walks slowly to me. She places her hand on the side of my face looking up into my eyes, "You, Ken, my love, are an angel. I must have known deep down. I love you, Kenneth Heart."

Our embrace and kiss fill me with loves desire. Now, I will know what only lovers know.

Chapter Thirteen
Town Of Angels Parade

Christmas Eve in Mystic Bay is everyone's favorite time. It's as if Santa himself sprinkled the town with cheer. Our annual parade is packed with residents and everyone is welcome. But this year it will be televised in the afternoon on The July North TV show. The celebration is in honor of the newly formed Angel Rescue Ranch. Yes, Mr. Dern Lumberton is a quiet hero in town now. A miracle happened the day Dern made the discovery of his uncles' letter. Dern read the letter to us at our Board meeting.

With tears in his eyes, the man with a newfound goal, strength and hope found his calling because of the letter:

Dear Dern,

I will be gone on to meet God when you read this. You know your Aunt Beatrice and I always wanted children. To be called Dad and Mother, well it would have been a blessing but it never happened. We hoped you'd want to come around sometimes, me especially, after my dear wife passed away.

I leave you this property hoping you might turn it into a rescue for animals. It is your choice though. If my hunch is right Mystic Bay will turn your head around someday and you will see what Beatrice and I saw. Angels appeared to the most vulnerable of children, those with special needs. For they, with purity of heart, could see the angels.

I wish you a good life. What I learned here was this, only kindness matters.

As I go to my Maker, please know your Aunt Beatrice and I forever will love you.

Uncle Zeke

Anyone can enter the parade with a decorated car or horse drawn wagon. There is never a disappointment in the effort every participant gives to shine. This year's parade is no exception. Horse drawn wagons and decorated convertibles are the floats. Leading the parade is Angel Gabe and Aunt Helen as Mr. and Mrs. Santa Claus. In clothes of red they ride in a horse drawn carriage made to look like a sleigh. And of course, Dawn, the recued dwarfed deer, is in the front with her little antlers and red coat! Even Bubbles, the squirrel, donning a red Santa hat, gets to ride on Gabe's shoulder chatting away as he usually does. The crowd lining the streets wave and yell as Christmas music plays for all to hear.

Second in line is the mayor and his wife in their truck packed with gifts. Behind them some of our beloved kids from our sports teams in their uniforms are waving to the crowd. We seven town angels take part in the parade by helping organizing it. Phil's Christmas trees line another horse drawn wagon lit to perfection and covered in faux snow. It's afternoon in the town but the street lights shine on the wreaths and banners that decorate the streets. There's a frosty the Snowman car, Ice Castle car and Toy Wagons car. July North and her sister, January, dressed in white velvet dresses with red sashes look like twins as July's voice and angelic face grace the Jumbotrons.

"What a world we live in," she says, "Where people come and share their love for Christmas, the holidays and giving."

Andy and his wife are in the next car with a few of their rescue dogs dressed for Christmas. Next a truck trailing a boat decorated like a Santa's sleigh with owner Jack, of Jack's by the Sea Restaurant with wife Stella wearing elf suits and waving. Hannah, Josh's wife, is in a car with a wagon piled with hay and behind it what every one of us has been waiting for, large cut out photograph signs of all the horses faces that were rescued. Twenty two volunteers carry the signs past the cheering crowd. July tells the millions of viewers and townsfolk, "Today, because of this town of angels, we see our rescue horses' twenty-two names written on the bottom of each sign below. Rudolph, Dasher, Dancer, Prancer, Vixen, Comet, Cupid. Donner, Blitzen, Noel, Star, Tinsel, Christmas, Snowflake, Snowball, Elf, Merry, Ribbon, Candy Cane, Sugar, Twinkle and Cookie. So many anonymous donors and volunteers made this charity happen." The cheers from the sidelines make my heart sing. Next is Justine's and my Butterfly and Angel Float. We enjoyed filling the float pulled by Klaus' car filled with everything Christmas butterfly and angel. Mac and Billie Jo and Val ride along waving. The second to last in the parade is my dear Jordana riding a black stallion, Midnight, she rescued just days ago. Midnight came to Jordana's outstretched arms. It was love at first sight, just like my love for Jordana. She waves. The cheering is almost deafening as everyone knows the new vet in town helped the animals move ever so quietly with her healing touch. They all didn't witness the miracle of the horses, though, as Jordana raised her hands to her side and closed her eyes, the timid, abused horses calmed, turned and followed her with loving confidence. This parade is as magical as Christmas butterfly and angel ornaments on decorated trees in the store windows. The vendors have plenty of food to eat along the street, hot cocoa, and hot cider are provided by the city and Christmas cookie stands are everywhere.

The last and final car pulls a wagon painted in imitation snow. On it is Benny Chen, the boy with a visual impairment who miraculously heard the angels sing him the song to play on his piano for the world. The piano has been placed on the wagon as he continually plays The Angels Song, Forever Love Forever Peace. His father, who plays violin in the San Francisco Orchestra quartet, accompanies him. Their wagon is trimmed with silver and white ornaments and bows.

When the TV show and parade end, we see Angel July singing the praises to the town she loves.

"Come to Mystic Bay anytime to see our new Angel Rescue Ranch and the lovely town that does so much. Our Angel Museum is in the wonderful next town over, Riverton. It's a charming town with an old fashioned feel. We are completing another horse rescue in Millersville. Christmas is about love and part of love is giving. Give to others, to children, to animals. Please give and your heart will be full.

Merry Christmas, everyone!"

Chapter Fourteen
December 26 – One Year Later

It's the day after Christmas and Walt has put a trellis of holly and poinsettias around the entrance to the Angel Rescue Ranch. It is here that nuptials will take place. The bride looks exceptionally heavenly wearing a white organza long dress. Her hair is swept in a ponytail with a red rose. The groom wears a black suit, white shirt and red tie to match the red rose in his bride's hair. The best man dons clothing colors the same as the grooms. Their dogs wear red ribbons as collars. The matron of honor wears a long dress of red satin.

Reverend Manuel again performs this ceremony as he did Christmas Eve at three yesterday before the Christmas parade. There walked down the aisle of The Garden Methodist Church my dear angel sisters, July and January marrying their wonderful guys, Klaus and Paul, respectively. The church was quiet with just a few friends but the reception in town square Christmas night included the whole town as guests. Music and laughter filled the air as punch and cookies quelled the guest's appetites. We all will have a private reception for the six of us at Klaus and now July's home on Sea Watch Hill in a few days. But today as the sky is filled with noonday and the clouds waft lazily by in the December blue sky we will marry.

Our vows are from our hearts of love:

"I, Kenneth Heart Leighton, take thee, Jordana May, to be my wife, my love for all eternity. I give to you my undying love, my angel sent to me from above.

My eyes fill with tears as Jordana says her vows. "You came into my life, an angel of a man, a protector of my heart. I give to you my undying love. And I vow to be the best mother to our son, Val." Val takes Jordana's hand and squeezes it. Mabel is wiping a tear yet smiling the biggest smile ever. The dogs, King, Honey and Little Guy doze now on the grass. The horses gaze at their sweet woman who helped change their world to a healthy one of safety and kindness. As we kiss the sky lights up with what only I can see, a plethora of angels singing for our union and for our town. Angel Claire sings with them standing by the horses, her blonde hair shimmering as her wings shine in the sunlight. The animals see her and come to her as she sprinkles them with angel dust of love. How I wish the whole world could see them. I thank God above for the blessings of this day. I see Madam Norma in the midst, her face smiling, her eyes filling with tears of joy.

Chapter Fifteen
Christmas Comes Again

We named our baby girl, May Norma Leighton. She is a beautiful little baby as all babies are. We adopted her, an orphan from Mexico.

Val thinks May looks just like him. Jordana stayed home with her as Val and I went to the Christmas parade. This time King, Honey and Little Guy went with us. When we tell people our eighty pound dog is named Little Guy, well, their eyes get big as the moon. But Mama Bear Jordana, as I call her now will be waiting for us rocking May. Mabel comes every Sunday for dinner and helps babysit for little May, too. We have our extended family of the seven angels and their families. But also, we have included Walt in family functions. He's another one of the town's great folk. He loves working at the bike store part time and as caretaker for the Angel Rescue Ranch and has many friends now.

His best buddy is Jamie Bond. He and Jamie sit with their dogs at night on the porch of Zeke's old farmhouse. Aunt Helen, Shari and Jordana fixed it up for Walt, who makes it his home now rent free. As we angels fly by many a Saturday night, Luna, Walt's rescue, and Bondo look up at us and we hear the men talk about angels.

"Those dogs got to be seeing something up there," Walt says seriously.

Jamie laughs, "Oh, believe me they are seeing angels. Sometimes I think I hear the sound of wings rushing like when geese fly by. Funny, but I swear I do."

"I know angels sent me Coach Ken and the people of Mystic Bay. Meeting the people of Mystic Bay, including you, changed my life. I'll be forever grateful, Jamie."

"Hey, Mystic Bay changed my life for the better, too. I finally became the man I was supposed to become," Jamie says.

Val and I watch the parade end as July North introduces the last vehicle in the parade. Val says, "Hey Dad look who's in Andy Walin's car float with the dogs. It's that Mr. Dern man, the guy that didn't want to help the horses but then he changed."

"I know Val, isn't it wonderful? It shows people can change no matter how unkind, how sad or afraid they are. When love encircles them and the angels are near, well, many times they see the light of love. But you know what Klaus did? He asked Mr. Dern to help him with the rescue ranch in Millersville that Klaus just opened. More horses are going there after the first of January. It's Mystic Bay's next mission."

"Wow, people are good, huh, Dad?"

Yes son," I say with my arm around his shoulder. "Most people have good in their hearts."

When the Christmas parade is over and Main Street is quiet still but gleaming with Christmas lights and the memory of laughter and cheer, I walk Val and our dogs to our home on twenty Moon Road. How I love this old house with the ever present memory of Madam Norma. I think Jordana is asleep so I tiptoe up the stairs with Val and dogs behind. I tuck my son in with Honey and Little Guy.

"Merry Christmas, Dad. Tomorrow after the presents, we go to see the horses, right?"

"Yes, Val, we go to wish our special horses a Merry Christmas, too with special treats. Then we'll stop over at Doc Lindley's Christmas party and see the deer and all the animals. Wow, we will have fun! Good night, I love you."

"Love you too."

I tiptoe into our bedroom with King trailing behind me. He settles into his own bed by the foot of our bed. May is asleep but Jordana is not. She sits in the rocker in her nightgown. In the rosy glow of the lamp, I find a worried look on her face.

Are you all, right? I walk over and stroke her head.

"Ken, there is something strange going on in my back. Feel this on both sides. She stands with her back to me and I feel her back. I release my hands and step back.

"What is it," she asks frightened?

"Sit down," I say. She sits on the bed and I sit beside her, my arms about her.

"This is something I've never seen but only heard about from July and January".

"What do you mean?" She starts to cry.

"Jordana, every once and awhile a human on earth becomes an angel. July and January became angels as children. They were abused but were taken away from their home. They found wonderful adoptive parents. To help them heal God made them angels. They brought cheer and stability to their new family's life and subsequently to so many. You are transitioning now into an angel.

"What? But why? Why me?" She is still frightened.

I smile as tears stream down her face.

"Don't be afraid. Heaven has chosen you for all you do helping animals and people, and for all you are, for the loving spirit inside you. You have become an angel living as human. Miracles happen, dear one. You can fly now. We will fly, you and I; we will help so many others everywhere we are needed. We will soar together and then one day when our children are old enough, we will tell them the story."

"We are angels doing God's work. We will tell them what has happened in Mystic Bay, how the town came together over many a year, helping so many to live a loving life. We will tell them the truth. Only love can mend the world, only love can mend a hurting heart. Only love can set us free."

Her wings spread out as she stands. They are made of light, sparkling like snowflakes in the sun. Angel Claire appears now and Jordana can see her guardian angel in real time not just in a dream this time. She communicates wordlessly, *Go sweethearts, go into the night. I will watch over the children til you return.*

Jordana's face fills with light as brilliant as her wings. Through the open window we fly in the night. Jordana's happiness brings music to my heart. Her smiling face is wide with excitement. The woman I love is now an angel on earth like me! We fly with the salty sea breeze at our backs, we are not cold, nor shivering in the night, but flying with laughter in our hearts, as a sweet screech owl named Boots, leads the way. To the horses we fly. Twenty-three wait for us under the glow of the milky Christmas moon.

Acknowledgements

With appreciation I thank Don McCauley, my publicist, for his wisdom, kind patience, and expertise. I thank Patty Mahoney, my friend, author and editor of four of my books. Patty edits with expert thoroughness and kindness. I thank author and illustrator, Susan Clare Anderson for her wonderful designs of Mystic Bay. I thank my family, husband, Dave, and my children, Mike and Elizabeth, and my sister, Karen, for their love and encouragement. I have met a few strangers who showed me kindness over the years. I have wondered if they could have been angels passing through my life. Angel Ken, and Val were two characters in my book that came from these encounters. As I grieved for my late daughter, Kate, I met a man in the course of two days, who I later realized was really an angel. His presence and comforting words were gifts from above. He became the inspiration for the angels living as humans in my Mystic Bay Series.

www.jodysharpe.com

Chapter 1   Madam Norma

Madam Norma's spirit appears before me. I'm Angel Ken, standing on a wintery day on the California beach near my home in quaint Mystic Bay. King, my loyal dog, as always, is by my side. Our town is known as the town of angels because a few years ago a miracle happened. Angels appeared to three children with special needs. Our seaside slice of heaven is also known for its community of good works, helping humans and animals alike. In the town are some with the gift of intuition.

Madam Norma was the oldest and wisest psychic in town. Before she went to heaven, she was my favorite earthly friend. Now in the heavenly realm, our friendship still remains strong. As she seemingly floats before me, she is young again as all are who go to heaven's realm. I see her spirit frequently and today as her blue eyes and favorite blue dress sparkle in the sunrise, she shows me a memory of her life. It's as if I'm seeing a glittery gold film before my eyes. King looks up and sees her as he was once her furry companion. Like me, he loves her still. Her filmy memory catches me in the glow of its beautiful story . . .

20 Moon Road, 1922 Mystic Bay

Madam Norma shows me the scene from her youth. It's bedtime in the Jarvis household at twenty Moon Road, Mystic Bay, California. Norma's parents Chuck and Leona Jarvis are asleep in their bed. They were the first couple to establish a business in the town of Mystic Bay. Chuck, bought an acre of land a block away from the coast in nineteen thirteen. He and Leona built their home and Mystic Bay's first grocery store. With twenty other families, they worked together, building the little seaside town around Main Street. With the sea breeze swirling around the white two story house with blue shutters, night is falling. Norma's Little sister, Emmy Lou, five, is tucked in her bed in the upstairs bedroom with her favorite white stuffed animal, Kitty. There is only a dim light from the bathroom across the hall. Nine year old, Norma, stands in the doorway. "Hello, Emmy Lou," she says quietly. Her nightgown is white dotted swiss, homemade by her mother's loving hands. Her auburn hair is swept into pigtails, mirroring her sister's.

"Hello, Emmy Lou, I'm your Good Fairy!"

Emmy Lou sits up, "No, you're not! You're my sister, Norma!"

"I look exactly like your sister, but I'm really your Good Fairy. I've come to tell you a story about an angel and a swan."

Emmy Lou looks in wonder as her sister sits gently on Emmy Lou's twin bed. "Now close your eyes and listen to the story." Emmy Lou closes her eyes as Norma creates a story for her sister. "Once upon a time, on a bright starry night when the moon was full, a beautiful golden haired angel wearing a pink flowing gown sat by a pond. With silvery wings at her side, she called to a black swan resting, his head tucked under his wing. The swan looked up at the angel and swam to the shore. The angel rose, her arms reached out to the swan. The swan flew up from the rippling water. Away they flew together into the night. They flew high as if flying up to the moon and stars."

As the story ends and Emmy Lou has fallen asleep, Norma can't believe her eyes. The angel in her made up story stands at the foot of the bed, her silvery wings fluttering. The angel communicates wordlessly and Norma somehow understands,

Norma, I am your guardian angel. I know you have seen me in your dreams many nights but now you are old enough to see me always. My dear Norma, you will do great things, you will become a pillar of the town, a woman with intuition and a sensitivity beyond what others have. You will see the future sometimes but most of all you will help people with the guidance of angels. Dear one, you will be the only one in town to see angels for many years. You can see angels now for there is only kindness in your heart.

Her memory for me ends and Madam Norma smiles communicating wordlessly, Write my story, my dear Angel Ken. Write the story of my life, my hundred years in Mystic Bay. For it is now that the world must know I saw angels. Please write how the angel's love guided me through my century of living. I will send you another memory soon. Madam Norma blows me a kiss, disappearing surprisingly as the angels do in a flicker of light. I walk home with tears flowing. I must write it all down for her, my dearest friend, for future generations.

Yes, I have a beautiful angel wife and two children. Yes, I own an angel store in town and run a sports program for disadvantaged youth. Yes, no one in town knows I'm an angel. Only Madam Norma knew I was an angel and told me so the day she passed on. For years she kept the secret safe that angels live as humans in Mystic Bay. For now, the secret is safe. Of course, I will write Madam Norma's story because as the intuitive woman knew, angels are everywhere.

I walk up the path behind Madam Norma's childhood home, 20 Moon Road, which is now my home. King and I walk in the back door of our cozy house filled with loving memories of Madam Norma and her family. As my wife and children sleep upstairs, I open my computer on the kitchen table and sit down to write. I look at King nestling in his dog bed, eyes closing in the morning sunshine coming through the window. My words start to flow.

20 Moon Road

The Psychic and the Angels

By Kenneth Leighton

Chapter 1   The Good Fairy and the Angel

20
moon
Road